MAGICAL MISTLETOE

by

Magnolia "Maggie" Rivers

Always believe in the magic!

Maggie Rivers

Published by

Freeman Group, L.L.C.
Des Moines, IA

Magical Mistletoe
by Magnolia "Maggie" Rivers

Published by Freeman Group, L.L.C.
Des Moines, IA

First Printing: February 2018

Print:
ISBN-13/EAN-13: 978-1-943793-06-8

E-book:
ISBN-13/EAN-13: 978-1-943793-07-5

Cover design: E.J. Whitmer

Printed in the United States of America

Dedication

To: You.

Yes, you. You picked up my book and hopefully bought it and are right now sitting in your favorite place about to begin reading a story I created for your reading pleasure. So, yes, this book is dedicated to you.

It is my hope, once you start reading this story, you absolutely cannot put it down until you reach "The End." You can hate me for that while you head off to work with no sleep (as I do when I write).

But really, I just appreciate the fact you've spent your hard-earned dollars purchasing one of my books. I appreciate you, my reader, whether this is the first book of mine you've purchased or your fourth or fifth.

I hope you enjoy it!

Love,

Maggie

P.S. I hope to meet you all in person someday!

Dedication
(continued)

To my son, J.D.

As always, you are the "wind beneath my wings".

From the first moment I saw you, you became the air I breathe. Without you, my world would cease to exist.

I love ya, babe! You are my hero.

I am so very, very proud of you!

To my daughter-in-law, Sheila

Thanks for making him happy.

In loving memory of my mother,
Vaudeen Freeman
(July 14, 1924 – November 5, 2009)
"Mama, I miss you daily."

THANKS TO

MAGGIE'S MAGICAL STREET TEAM!

Yeah! You ladies and gents rock! Thanks to all of you for helping me name the fictitious town of Shady Rivers. And a huge thank you for helping me decide what types of stores should be in the town and the name of the stores! It was a tough call on some of them. So thanks to:

Liz Gough – town name of Shady Rivers
Barb Hooten – South & Son's Mechanic Garage
Brenda Sullivan – Bo's Bar
Tina Bixler - Dottie's 5 & 10
Darrel Day – This & That Second Hand Shop
Bill Sanford – Becky's Bakery
Francie Rose Wright-Carr – Wright's Hardware
Linda Johnson – Katy's Kitchen
Shir-Lee Miskimen – Hales Grocery Store
Brenda Sullivan – Tuckerman's Barber Shop
Ellen Waldrop – Sweet Strings Dulcimer Shop
Janice Barrentine – Daisy's Tattoo Shop
Peggy DuPré – The Cat's Meow Artist Studio

Many, many thanks. Hope you enjoy "our" town and its inhabitants as much as I have!

THANKS TO

Jeff L. Makemson
Supervising Wildlife Biologist – District III
Alabama Division of Wildlife and Freshwater Fisheries

A huge thank you to Jeff Makemson for sharing your vast knowledge of the North American Bison with me. Your help in creating "Tiny," the buffalo you'll find in the fictitious town of Shady Rivers, Alabama, was invaluable.

For my readers, please keep in mind, that "Tiny" is a figment of my imagination and therefore any discrepancies between his actions and those of a true, real life North American Bison are totally from the Author's imagination and in no way should they reflect on Mr. Makemson's expertise.

As the saying goes, you can "lead a horse to water but you can't make him drink." Mr Makemson gave me the information I needed so my Author's imagination could take over and create "Tiny." I hope you enjoy reading about him as much as I enjoyed creating him.

Thank you again, Jeff, for your help.

MAGICAL MISTLETOE

By

Magnolia "Maggie" Rivers

CHAPTER ONE

"What is it with you damn women anyway?" mumbled Spencer Cartwright tugging at the inebriated woman as he tried to get her down from the large basswood tree growing on the town square.

"I-I can't do-o-o-o th-this," replied the woman, her tongue sounding three sizes too large for her mouth. "I-I'm afraid of heights. O-o-o-o-o-hhhhhhh it's so-o-o-o far down there," she said as she clung tightly to the tree's trunk while squishing her eyes shut.

Spencer pinched the bridge of his nose and dragged his hand down his face in frustration at yet another drunken tourist who thought it was perfectly okay to ignore the posted rules of his quaint little Southern town.

It never failed. Every December during Shady Rivers' Christmas Artisan Festival time, the looneys came out of the woodwork to try to steal a piece of mistletoe off that damnable tree. Some years he would like nothing better than to just chop the thing down himself and be done with it, but the townsfolk loved their tree. Dang that

3

newspaper for spreading that tidbit of folklore in the first place.

He knew there was no such thing as magical mistletoe but some enterprising person had started that rumor years ago. The silly rumor had spread by word of mouth alone and tourists flocked to their small town making business for the locals good. Some made enough to carry them from year to year.

"Look, Miss, you're not gonna fall. You're really close to the ground. But, if you keep trying to climb this tree in those spiky shoes you have on, you're definitely gonna break your neck and the closest hospital is over in Tuscaloosa. Now, listen, I'm right here. So, come on. Just pick up your foot and move it down."

"You're cute," she said as she opened her eyes and looked down at Spence, her breasts level with his head.

"Great, just great," said Spence as his gaze locked on the outline of her jacket covered perfectly rounded breasts. He hooked his thumbs over his belt to keep from reaching up to palm them in his hands. "Hold on," said Spence as he reached up and grabbed her around the waist, pulling her toward him. She smelled delicious. "Turn loose of the limb. I've got you."

"I might fall!"

"I'm standing on the ground, for Pete's sake. Turn loose."

"I-I can't. I'm scared," she said as she clung tighter to the tree.

"Hey, look at me. Just look how cute I am. Look at these muscles," he said as he flexed his right arm.

The woman gazed down at him.

"Go ahead, squeeze my arm. You know you want to. Go ahead." *Damn, what beautiful green eyes.*

"Oooooohhhhh," the woman said as she turned loose of the limb with one hand and reached down to touch Spence's arm.

Grabbing her tighter, he pulled her off the tree and stood her on the ground. *Feels so nice.*

"This feels like steel," she said squeezing his bicep with both hands. "You're cute, did I tell you that?"

"I'm glad you think so. Now, I'm afraid I'm going to have to take you to jail for public intox," he said reaching around and grabbing the cuffs off his duty belt. *Wonder if she's ever seen the inside of a jail cell?*

"Jail? I can't go to jail. No-o-o-o, can't do that. You have the cutest dimple," said the woman as she clung to Spence trying to keep her balance.

"Sorry, Miss, but I need your name," said Spence trying to keep his mind on business and the stiffness out of his man parts. Even through her clothes he could feel the softness of her well-proportioned body.

"Shhhhhh, don't tell anyone. I have to have a piece of that magical mistletoe. Did you know it's ma-ma-magical?"

"No, you can't be climbing up the tree. See that sign right there," he said as he pointed in the sign's direction. "Besides, it's not magical. That's just an ol' wives' tale. There is no such thing as magical mistletoe. You'd do well to keep that in mind," he said as he tried to steady the woman as she kept wobbling in the stilettos she was wearing. It was a wonder she didn't break her neck just walking in those things. But he did like the looks of her tiny little feet in them. Sexy just about covered it.

"I beg your par, par, pardon but yes, there is. That mistletoe up there is magical. My grandmother told me so. And my grandmother never lied," she declared as she pulled her light jacket tighter.

"Well, I'm sure she didn't but you can't have the mistletoe and I have to take you in. Now what's your name?"

What was it about the Christmas season that brought out the stupidity in people? It was just an old wives' tale and people with any amount of intelligence should know there's no such thing as magical mistletoe because there was no such thing as magic.

"You m-m-mean you don't know who I am?"

"No, I'm afraid I don't. Your name, please ma'am."

"I'm the Honorable J-J-J-Judge Abigail Rutledge. So, see, you can't arrest me," she said as she laid her head against his chest and draped her arms around his neck. "You smell nice. I like you."

"Well, I still need to put these cuffs on you," said Spence as he tried pulling one of her arms from around his neck.

"Ohhhhh," she said as tears began to trickle down her cheeks, "but, you can't. I told you, if New York gets wind of this I'll be out of a job. 'Judge gets arrested in Podunk City for drinking too much.' Now how would that look on my record?"

You should have thought of that before you got snockered and climbed up this tree.

6

"I'm sorry ma'am," said Spence as he snapped the cuffs around her wrists.

"But, you don't understand. I have to be sure. I just can't marry him without being sure. I mean, geez, you'd think I'd know, but, see, this is why that mistletoe is the answer."

"Listen, I'm sorry you have boyfriend troubles, but that mistletoe is not going to help you in that department." Grabbing hold of her upper arm, Spence steadied her on her feet.

"No, no, you're wrong."

"That whole thing about it being magical is an ol' wives' tale and it's not true. There is no such thing as magic and this is just plain ol' mistletoe. It's a fungus plant. All it's good for is to get people hurt when they fall out of the tree."

"You're wrong. That's how my grandmother knew. She picked a piece of that mistletoe when she was sixteen. She was standing right here holding it in her hand and looking at that tree," said Abby as she faced the tree. "When she turned around, there was my grandfather. Of course, he wasn't my grandfather then, but she told me all about it. How their eyes met, and he walked up to her and asked her to have a soda with him right over there in that little café. They were married for fifty-two years. She always told me when I wanted to find Mr. Right I could find him right here with a piece of that mistletoe up there."

"Well, Miss, that all sounds nice but it sounds like what you call a coincidence to me."

"No, please, I have to know. I can't get married without knowing if he's Mr. Right," said Abby as the tears continued.

7

"I'm sure that's something you'll know when the time comes."

"But see, that's the problem. I don't know. We've been engaged for five years. He says he wants to get married right away. But, I don't know. Deep down, I don't know if this is the guy I want to spend the rest of my life with, have kids with and grow old together. How do you really know?"

"You're asking the wrong person. Listen, that piece of greenery isn't going to help with that either. See, I've been told, if you don't feel he's Mr. Right, as you call him, right here," said Spence as he thumped his chest, "then he's not the right one. Tell you what I'm gonna do, it's almost Christmas. Oh, wow! Look at that," Spence continued, holding his palm out, "It's beginning to snow."

"But it can't snow. It's way too warm."

"Yeah, it's warm down here but higher up it's colder. It'll melt just about the time it hits the ground. I haven't seen a measurable snow here since, well, in about twenty years."

"Oh quick, catch it on your tongue and make a wish," said Abby as she opened her mouth and tried to pull away from Spence.

"Now what on earth is that supposed to do?" he asked as he held her arm to keep her from falling.

"My grandma said when you catch the first snowflake on your tongue, you make a wish and your wish comes true." Sticking her tongue out, she caught a snowflake.

"Surely, as a judge, you don't believe in such nonsense."

"My grandma never lied to me," she replied as she made a face and stuck her tongue out at Spence.

Mercy but this woman was trying his patience and turning him on at the same time. He wanted to put his lips on hers and suck that little tongue deep into his mouth.

"Maybe not, but she sure told some tall tales. So, listen, here's what I'm gonna do," said Spence as he removed the cuffs from her wrists. "Where do you live?"

"Why?"

"Instead of taking you to jail, I'm going to take you home. You're too drunk to drive yourself. How many drinks have you had anyway?"

"One. I had one. Oh wait, maybe it was two. Three. Yes, three. I think."

"Well, if that's all, you must not be able to hold your liquor very well," said Spence as he guided her toward his truck."

"Guess not, but th-then I don't drink. I'm a judge."

"I see. Well, it's too cold for you to walk so give me your address. I'll take you home but you must promise me not to try this little stunt again. I know what kind of damage this'll do to your career if it got out. So, we'll just consider it a 'pay it forward' and some day you can pass it along to some poor slob in your courtroom."

Abby stood there, wiping at the tears on her cheeks, looking at the officer.

"I, I don't think you told me your name?" she said.

"It's Spencer. Most people just call me Spence," he replied as he reached up to brush away a tear from her cheek but quickly caught himself and dropped his hand back to his side. "Come on," he said as he took her by the arm, "let's get you in my truck and get you home before you freeze out here."

Helping her into his vehicle, he walked around and slid into the driver's seat.

"Where's your patrol car?"

"Town can't afford one, so you get to ride in my truck. Now where do you live?"

"Arlington Street. Three sixty-two Arlington Street."

Spence turned toward her, resting his left arm on the steering wheel.

"You're that woman next door?"

Abby stared back at him.

"You're the woman who moved into Mrs. Rutledge--, you're Mrs. Rutledge's daughter?"

"Yes, no, I mean Ethel Rutledge if that's who you're referring to is my grandma," said Abby as she leaned her head against the truck's window.

"You're my neighbor?"

"If you're th-that hunky guy I keep seeing coming and go-going from the house next to me, then I guess I am. I've had sex with you every night since I've been here. You're a hunk. I love your sh-shaved head. I grab you by the ears and ..." Abby closed her eyes.

A moment later, Spence heard a slight snore.

"Dang," he said, "sure hope I enjoyed all that sex." This woman was going to be one embarrassed judge come daylight. Smiling, he turned back in his seat, buckled his seat belt, cranked the truck and pulled away from the curb.

CHAPTER TWO

Spence pulled into Abby's drive and parked. Glancing over at the still sleeping woman, he realized she must have her housekey stuck down in her jeans pocket.

"Miss, Miss," he said as he shook her shoulder gently. "Miss, I need you to wake up. I need your housekey."

Abby mumbled in her sleep and pushed at his hand as she pulled her legs up underneath her and settled back down.

Spence looked through the windshield glancing from her house to his a few hundred yards away. Putting the truck in reverse, he backed out of her drive and pulled into his a few minutes later. Shutting off the vehicle, he got out, walked onto his porch and unlocked the front door.

Returning to his truck, he opened Abby's door, catching her in his arms as she slowly fell outward.

Lifting Abby in his arms, Spence carried her through his front door, kicking it closed behind him. He stood for a moment, trying to decide what to do with her, before taking her up the stairs and into his bedroom.

Laying her into his bed, he stood back up and glanced down at her as her soft snores continued.

Might better take off the coat and shoes.

After removing her coat, he grabbed hold of her stilettos and pulled them off. He placed them on the floor underneath the edge of the bed, pulled the covers up over her, and tucked her in. He stood there for a moment shaking his head. *Damn woman could have killed herself trying to climb that stupid tree in those things.* He felt a jolt of something. *Damn fine-looking woman is all I can say.*

Closing the bedroom door, Spence returned to his truck and drove back to the town square.

For a few minutes, he stood in front of the basswood tree looking up at the mistletoe growing in the top.

"Damn fungus," he muttered. "Some people are just stupid. And her a judge. Like a damn fungus is gonna bring two people together. Hmmmph."

Spence shook his head, turned and walked back to his truck. Climbing in, he settled in for the night's watch. Pouring himself a hot cup of coffee from his thermos, he watched the snowflakes falling on the square for the first time in years.

As if on cue, he spotted Tiny rambling down the street toward him. Spence knew what the big bison wanted so, reaching over to the glove compartment, he opened it and pulled out an apple. He bit off a bite for himself then held the rest out of the truck's window just as Tiny arrived. The big animal gently took it from Spence's hand and chewed in contentment.

"Well, fellow, at least you don't give me any trouble over that damnable mistletoe," said Spence as he scratched behind the bison's ears. "Go on now. I'll bet Miss Katy's got a piece of fried apple pie saved back there just for you."

As if he understood Spence's every word, Tiny lumbered off leaving Spence alone again.

* * *

Abby awoke with a pounding headache. Rolling over, she glanced for the clock on her nightstand. It wasn't there. On second glance, neither was *her* nightstand. Her head pounded harder. Something was off kilter.

Glancing around the room, she noted the unfamiliar shades on the windows. Where were her curtains? And the walls. Someone had removed her beautiful lavender flowered wallpaper. There was something wrong here. This furniture was not hers.

She sat straight up in bed. Her ears pounded with a swishing noise, her stomach flipped and her mouth tasted as though she'd been chewing on rubber tires. There must be an eighteen-wheeler around because she'd definitely been run over by one. The memory from last night flooded back into her still groggy brain.

Oh, dang, why on earth do people get drunk?

Abby threw the cover back and swung her feet off the side of the bed. A wave of nausea swept over her. *And people drink that disgusting*

13

stuff every day. Just wait'll I get another drunk in my courtroom.

She sat on the side of the bed looking down at her clothing.

Still dressed. That's a plus. Oh, dang, what did I say! Last night's episode continued to return in bits and pieces.

Slipping on her jacket and picking up her shoes, she quietly walked across the floor and slowly opened the bedroom door. Peeking out, she saw no one. The smell of coffee permeated the air. Her stomach complained even more.

Silently she crept down the hallway to the top of the stairs. She still saw no one in sight. *This might just be my lucky day.* Hurriedly she tiptoed down the stairs toward her escape.

"In a hurry?" asked a male voice from behind her as she reached for the knob on the front door.

Damn. So close yet so far.

"Uh, no. I just didn't want to wake anybody," she replied.

"Oh, you didn't wake me. It's noon."

"Noon? You've got to be kidding me. I've never slept until noon in my life. Early bird gets the worm and all that..."

"I guess you missed the worms this morning but I've got some toast. That'll probably help your stomach. At least I assume your stomach's a little queasy this morning."

"More like a lot, if you ask me. My head is pounding. Why do people drink that stuff anyway?"

"Well, I hear some people drink it for courage to climb trees when they're afraid of heights in the first place." Spence raised his cup of coffee to his mouth to hide the grin spreading across his face.

"This is embarrassing."

"Well, I'm afraid it gets a lot worse." Spence turned and walked back into the kitchen. "Come on. I'll fix you that toast before you go."

"Worse? Oh shit, what did I do?" Abby asked as she slowly made her way into the kitchen behind Spence, her head throbbing with each step.

"I'm sure the evening's activities will come back to haunt you at some point. They usually do."

"You sound like you've had experience with hangovers before." Abby plopped down at the small kitchen table and propped her head in her hands.

"This time of year, I seem to arrest my fair share of drunks. Here," said Spence as he placed a glass on the table in front of her. "Drink this."

Abby opened one eye and glanced at the red liquid.

"Looks like tomato juice," she said.

"Tomato juice, with some cayenne pepper, sugar and a little lime added."

"Is that an ol' wives' tale to cure hangovers?"

"Nope. It'll keep you hydrated and clean out some of the poison you drank last night. Go on, drink up, you'll feel better."

"I'd have to die to feel better."

"Eat this. Maybe it'll soak up some of the booze." Spence sat a plate of toast on the table in front of her.

"I'm not sure it'll stay down."

15

Spence walked over to the counter and picked up a small jar.

"Tell you what. Let me see if I can get rid of the headache for you first, then maybe the toast will stay down," he said as he returned to the table unscrewing the lid on the jar.

"What *IS* that stuff?" Abby asked as she caught the scent of the potent smelling salve.

"Tiger Balm. You just close your eyes and relax as much as you can. I'm going to massage this into the back of your neck. It stings the eyes though so keep 'em closed for a few minutes and drink the tomato juice."

Spence stuck his fingers in the salve and moving Abby's long red hair to the side, he began massaging the back of her neck. *Soft hair. I could get use to soft hair.* Where did those thoughts keep coming from? It wasn't like him at all. He'd learned his lesson well years ago.

"Oh, but that feels heavenly," said Abby as the muscles in her neck began to relax. "I could use you back in New York during some of my trials."

Spence laughed.

Something inside Abby's heart slipped sideways at the sound.

"I'll bet a courtroom gets pretty interesting at times."

"Sometimes. But I'm an administrative law judge." *Calloused hands. Wouldn't expect a cop to have calloused hands.* "For the most part, it's boring stuff."

Spence dipped more salve from the jar, smeared it onto his fingers and began massaging Abby's temples.

"Drink your juice. It'll help."

16

"Listen, I really do appreciate your rescuing me last night and for taking care of me this morning."

"It's the least I could do after all the sex we've had."

CHAPTER THREE

Abby choked, spitting out the swallow of juice which she'd just taken.

"Wh-what?" she sputtered as she grabbed the napkin beside her plate and dabbed at her mouth before wiping the table.

Spence chuckled at her indignation. He liked this woman. Teasing her was going to be fun.

"Yeah, I wouldn't mind trying some of those kinky things again," he said as he resumed massaging her temples.

"What? We didn't, you better not have—"

"Cool your jets, darlin'," said Spence as he laughed. "You were just babbling on the way here last night and if I remember correctly you said, and I quote, 'I've had sex with you every night since I've been here. You're a hunk.'"

"Just shoot me now. I'm going to die of embarrassment anyway."

"No need to get embarrassed. I'll take it as a compliment. Just wait till I tell the guys at the bar I got a hot looking judge lusting after my hunky body parts."

"Oh, my lord! I don't suppose there's any way you could just forget I ever said that?"

"Well, let me see now. What's it worth to you?" he asked as he walked over to the kitchen sink and washed the Tiger Balm off his hands.

Swallowing the last of the tomato juice, Abby asked, "Isn't that considered black mail? And by a cop, no less."

"Only if I get caught. Isn't that how your clientele thinks?"

"Actually, I believe that's the problem. They don't think in the first place."

"Well, tell you what, any time you'd like to try out that sex thing, my door is always open."

"That's comforting to know. Now, I really need to get going. My headache is much better thanks to you and my stomach does seem to have settled down some. Thank you for taking care of me. I've never had a hangover before so I wouldn't have known about all this stuff to do for it." Abby stood and began walking to the door.

"How about if I treat you to dinner tonight?" Spence blurted out. "I mean, you're all by yourself over there in your grandma's house and all. I cook a mean steak on the grill."

Where had that come from? He wasn't in the habit of inviting women to his place. As a matter of fact, he wasn't in the habit of inviting women anywhere. Women were too messy for his taste. Oh sure, he indulged his desires when necessary, but he was very careful when he did. Always went to the big city where he wasn't known. Less messy that way. Never the same woman twice. Take a woman out on a date and they became clingy and tried to own you. He'd seen it all too often.

"Actually, that sounds great. You sure you don't mind?"

"Not at all. I like to cook and cooking for one gets boring. So, you'd actually be doing me a favor."

Spence opened the front door.

"In that case, how about if I bring the salad?"

"It's a plan. Seven okay?"

"I can do that," said Abby as she stepped out on the porch.

"I'll run you over to your place in my truck. You'll sink in the slush with those spiky shoes on.

"That's not necessary. I can take my shoes off when I get inside."

"I insist. The little bit of snow we got last night just turned into mud and muck. I was gonna head out to get a Christmas tree anyway, so I'll drop you off on the way."

"In that case, thanks."

* * *

An hour later, Spence stood in front of a seven-foot evergreen. He loved coming out to the old home place. That was the first thing he'd bought when he moved back. The old house was gone now. The basement was still there underneath the sod. He had bulldozed it full of dirt then planted grass seed on top. Less costly that way.

But, on the bright side, the wood from the house had been put to good use and a beautiful piece of it now sat in his living room thanks to Elmer Shelton, the best luthier around.

"Time to get down to business," said Spence as he began to saw into the trunk at the base of the tree.

Memories flooded back as he worked. After his stepdad disappeared, things changed. He and his mom went all out for Christmas. They had walked through these woods looking for just the perfect tree and when they found just the right one, he would cut it down and together they'd drag it back to the house. While he nailed boards onto the base of it to hold it up, his mom always made hot chocolate to warm them up. They'd spend the rest of the day talking, laughing, drinking chocolate and decorating the tree and the house for Christmas. Those were the good memories that caused an ache in his heart.

"Timber!" he bellowed to himself as it began to fall. He could hear his mom's laughter. He looked up toward Heaven and smiled.

An hour later, with the tree standing in its place in the living room, its pungent odor permeating the house, Spence headed to the basement to bring up the decorations.

CHAPTER FOUR

A few minutes before seven, Spence heard his doorbell ring followed by his front door opening.

"Spence, it's me," Abby called out, as she stood just inside.

"Who's me?" yelled Spence.

"It's me, Abby."

"Abby? Abby who?"

"Oh, you!" she said as she chuckled, closing the door behind her. An odd feeling of coming home settled over her.

"Welcome to my humble abode," said Spence, drying his hands on a hand towel as he walked out of the kitchen.

Abby laughed as she caught sight of his black bib apron with a picture of a car careening down a road, a possum in its headlights and the words 'Road Kill Café' written in red on the front.

"I do hope you bought those steaks at the grocery store."

"Now why would I do that when there's perfectly good stuff out there on the road, free for the taking."

"I may live in New York, but I was born and raised right here. I've eaten a lot of wild meat. Deer, turkey, turtle and all that stuff but I draw the line on roadkill." She laughed. "And no, possum on the half shell either."

Spence liked the way those green eyes lit up when she laughed. There it was again, that jolt of something. He couldn't quite put his finger on it but he'd figure it out later.

"Come on into the kitchen. Everything's just about ready. Here, let me take that bowl for you," he said as he took the big bowl of salad out of her hands. "And what the hell is possum on the half shell?"

"Don't tell me you haven't heard that before."

"Nope, afraid I haven't."

"Well, it's possum served on an armadillo shell." She laughed as she followed Spence into the kitchen. "What can I do to help?"

"Well, how about if you fix the drinks. I'll take some tea. It's in the fridge. Glasses are above the sink. Help yourself to whatever you'd like," he said as he picked up the plate with the steaks and headed toward the back door.

"Is the tea sweet?"

"Girl, you're in the South."

"Oh, sweet tea is fine for me, too," she said as she headed around the breakfast bar to get the glasses. "They just don't make it sweet in New York."

"Great, I'll toss these on and be right back," he said as he walked out the back door, shutting it behind him.

Moments later, Spence returned inside. His breath caught as he watched Abby moving around

24

his kitchen. A thought of belonging crept through his brain. She was beautiful in a plain sort of way. He could definitely get used to this scene. Thoughts of taking her on the countertop raced through his mind.

"Hope you like baked broccoli," he said as he tried to push those thoughts from his head.

"Yes, I do," replied Abby, as she poured tea into the glasses.

"How about your steak? How do you like it?"

Her eyes produced a startling contrast to her flame red corkscrew hair cascading down beyond her shoulders. Again, certain images flitted across his mind.

"Medium well is fine with me."

"Great! I'm a medium man myself so I can toss yours on first. That'll make it easy." Spence reined in his thoughts and picked up a pan of French bread, opened the oven door, removed the broccoli and placed the bread inside. He quickly removed the wrap from the top of the salad bowl and placed it on the bar before heading back outside.

"I'll go flip the steaks and be right back. I'll let you dish up the broccoli into that bowl there."

"I can do that."

Abby sat the two glasses of tea on the bar next to the plates Spence had set out, turned and picked up the bowl and dished up the broccoli before grabbing the oven mitt and taking the toasted bread from the oven.

"And here we are," said Spence as he returned inside with the two steaks on a platter.

"Those smell delicious and I'm starved," said Abby.

"Good. I like a woman who eats more than a bird," he said as he dished the steaks on the plates before setting the platter into the sink.

"You wouldn't like the women I work with then. They're all skinny as a rail and I swear they must eat nothing but bird seed." She laughed as she took her seat at the bar.

"So, how did you end up in New York in the first place?" asked Spence as he sat down across the bar from Abby.

"Oh, I don't know. Guess I was bored with small town living."

"Dig in before any of this gets cold. And save some room for dessert later."

"Dessert. Don't tell me you made dessert, too," she said as she took a bite of her steak.

"No, I can't take credit for that. But Becky's Bakery makes the best cheesecake on earth."

"Oh, my goodness. That woman must be a hundred years old!"

Spence laughed.

"No, no. If memory serves me Mrs. Becky just celebrated her ninety-first birthday. Her daughter, Elli, runs the bakery now but Mrs. Becky still goes to work every morning." Spence took another bite and picked up his glass of sweet tea.

"That's probably what keeps her going. I swear if I'd stayed here instead of going to New York, they'd have to put 'Death by Cheesecake' on my tombstone."

Spence laughed.

"Yours and everybody else's within a hundred miles." If she'd grown that lush body by eating cheesecake, he'd have to see that she had a continuous supply. Her breasts looked firm and round. A perfect match to her hips. His pants tightened a notch causing him to shift in his seat. "So, small town girl goes to the Big Apple and becomes a judge. Do you like it there?" He took a swallow of his tea and sat the glass back down.

"Yeah and no. I mean, it's an exciting city. There's always something to do no matter what time of the day or night. But, there's a part of me that misses home. You know, the slow pace, the quietness of country living. Looking out my kitchen window and watching nature. You just can't find that in the big city. I miss it. Seems like I miss it more as the years go by."

"So why don't you move back. You've got your grandma's house and all."

"I'm actually getting married."

"Sounds to me like you've got a case of cold feet about this marriage thing."

"In a way, I guess I do. I just want to be sure he's the right one."

"I would have thought you would have known that before you said yes."

"I thought I knew but the closer it gets to the day, the less I seem to be sure. I mean, he's a nice guy. Has a great job and all..."

"I hear a but."

"Oh, I don't know. I want a marriage that lasts. I have three really close friends in New York and they've all been married and divorced at least once. One is on her second husband and another her third. I don't want that. I want what my grandmother and my mother had. I want a guy who loves me for the duration. I want to be sitting in rocking chairs on our front porch when we're in our eighties watching our great grandchildren play. Oh goodness," she said, "just listen to me run off at the mouth."

27

"It's okay. I like listening to you," said Spence as he took another drink of his tea. He'd really like doing more than just talking. What he really wanted was to press his lips against hers and feel her tremble. "It sounds like you had a great childhood."

"I did. I was surrounded by family and lots of love. I want that again," said Abby as she ate the last bite of her steak.

"Sounds like the perfect storybook life."

"I guess it does, doesn't it?" Abby dabbed at her mouth with her napkin.

Spence watched the napkin touch her lips. *I could lick that off.* Damn those thoughts. Everything this woman did seemed to let those stray thoughts slip into his brain. He didn't understand.

"Guess I just don't believe in fairy tales."

Abby drew back in surprise. "You mean you don't believe in committing to another person?"

"Time has a way of eroding the good stuff and leaving the bad and marriages break apart from there."

"Not if you're really committed to each other. My own parents and grandparents proved that."

"So, you're committed to this guy you're about to marry. Is he committed to you?"

Abby's lips parted to answer then she stopped, an odd expression crossed her face.

"Mistletoe isn't going to help you find that answer," said Spence as he stood up. "How about if I clear up these dishes and pour us a glass of wine. We can sit in the sunroom and watch the 'coons come out."

"You have raccoons visiting your yard?"

"Yep. They're a nightly visitor. Probably because I feed them." He laughed as he picked up dishes and headed for the dishwasher.

"Oh, my goodness. What do you feed them?" asked Abby as she gathered up some of the dishes and walked them over to the sink.

"Well, they like nuts and grains. That type of thing. They also eat pet food. What they really like is marshmallows though. But, I don't give those to them very often. I save those for special occasions. I'll leave out a few for them on Christmas Eve."

"I'll just bet they love you, too."

"Don't know about that but they sure love the marshmallows."

Spence uncorked the bottle of wine and poured a couple of glasses. Handing one to Abby, he grabbed the other along with the bottle and motioned for her to head out to the sunroom ahead of him.

Spence liked the view from his position. Abby had the cutest butt in jeans. Tight and looked almost heart-shaped. He could certainly get used to that view. He'd like to know what it felt liked spooned against him with his hands cupping her breasts. Dang it! He needed to get those thoughts out of his brain or his body's physical reaction would betray his thoughts.

Abby sat down in one of the padded rockers and sat her wine glass on the end table next to it. She liked the looks of his sunroom. Most men would have turned it into a pool room with racks of pool cues hanging on every wall. Not this room though. Lots of potted plants, white walls and splashes of lemon colored material covering the wicker furniture. Definitely a woman's touch. Abby wondered who were the women in his life.

"Usually," said Spence as he took the rocker beside her, "they come from that direction over there," he said as he pointed towards a grouping of lilac bushes bordering the side of the yard. "This time of year though, they don't come out every night but I leave plenty of food out just in case."

Spence took a hefty sip of his wine. Catching a glimpse of movement in the direction of the bushes he pointed. "There," he said, "there's our first visitor. That one I call Wilson."

"Why Wilson?"

"After the volleyball in the Tom Hanks' movie. I had just moved into this house and he was the first visitor I had. We just kinda became friends. When nobody's around, he'll come up and take treats from my hand."

"He's cute."

"Maybe, but I leave them all out there. Don't want them moving into the house and I only put out food during the winter months when their food supply is a little scarce."

"That's probably a smart move."

"I'm not sure if it's smart or not but I figure they need to stay in the wild as much as possible. Wilson here, though, doesn't play by my rules. He's his own man. Comes around all year long lookin' for handouts."

"Typical male," said Abby as she laughed. She sat her wine glass on the table. This man was easy to talk to, unlike Preston who was all about himself. She needed to just sit down and make a list of all the things she liked about Preston. Maybe that would get rid of her cold feet.

"Penny for your thoughts," said Spence.

"Just thinking I need to get going. I have to clean out my grandma's house while I'm here and get it ready to sale."

"So you've made up your mind then. You're staying in the big city."

"I guess so. That's where my life is now."

"Maybe you just need to keep your grandma's house as a safety net," said Spence as he held up the wine bottle offering to pour her another glass.

Abby held up her glass and motioned for him to pour just a little bit.

"I just mean you'd always have some place to go for some down time. But then, you could always rent it out, too."

"I suppose. But Preston thinks it's better if we sell it. He says it's dead weight for what we want to accomplish."

"What do you think?"

"Oh, I don't know. I think I've just gotten cold feet lately. I just need to get on with our plans. Once I get through the wedding, things will calm down, I'm sure."

"If you say so," said Spence as he finished his glass of wine.

"Thank you for a wonderful evening. You're a great cook and pleasant company. I've enjoyed it," said Abby as she stood.

"So have I," said Spence. "It's nice to have someone to enjoy a glass of wine with me."

You're in trouble, ol' man. This woman is going to turn you inside out before she's on a plane and headed back to the Big Apple.

Spence took Abby's glass and set them both back down on the table as he guided her back to the front door.

"Thank you for a lovely evening," said Abby as she stopped at the doorway.

Spence took her coat from the rack and held it up as she slipped her arms through it.

"No, thank you," said Spence as he slipped on his own coat as he opened the door. "Let me walk you back to your place."

"Oh goodness, you don't have to do that."

"I always see a lady home," said Spence. "After all, you may be next door but that's about two city blocks away. A lot could happen in that distance. I mean, a bear could come out of nowhere and ask you for some porridge or something."

Abby laughed as she stepped outside. "Well, heavens-to-Betsy, we don't want that to happen, now do we. And do you have a bowl of porridge just in case?"

"I could whip one up real fast if I needed it," he said grinning.

"I'll just bet you could."

Spence reached over, took hold of her hand and placed it on his arm as he walked toward her house.

Abby's hand felt the warmth of his arm and her skin tingled. It felt nice. Even the coldness against her face made her senses seem more alive than they had been in a long time. Maybe it was just being back at home again and, then again, it might just be something else.

"Here you are," said Spence as he guided Abby up the steps onto her porch a few minutes later.

"Thank you again," she said.

"The pleasure was all mine," said Spence as he took her housekey and opened her door. Handing the key back to her, he bent down and placed a quick kiss on top of her head. "Good night. Oh, and let me know anytime you want a repeat of that wild monkey sex we seem to be having in your dreams."

Abby's mouth fell open. Before she could think of an answer, he was off the porch and on his way back home. Whistling as he went.

CHAPTER FIVE

Morning came early in Shady Rivers. Flo Johnson opened the doors of Flo's Beauty Boutique promptly at seven in the morning five days a week. She prided herself on serving the best cup of coffee in town, which was questionable by some, along with all the gossip you could handle.

"What do you mean? She was a he?" asked Agnes Moorhead as she seated herself underneath the hairdryer.

"Yes, that's it exactly. And I guess Bubba didn't know it. Sandra said they'd just had an hour or so of wild monkey sex and I guess poor Bubba was head over heels in love." Flo adjusted the hairdryer heat settings and set the timer.

"Well my goodness, what happened?"

"I guess Bubba proposed to her, I mean him, er her, Jonette! He proposed to Jonette." Flo threw her hands in the air in frustration.

"Oh my Lord, is he gonna marry her, him?" asked Agnes as she cocked her head from under the dryer in order to hear better.

"I don't know. Now you know Bubba, he may look like a mean, tough biker dude sitting

35

there on his Harley, them tattoos and that beard, but he's just a big ol' teddy bear, unless you get him riled."

"So that's why he's in jail?"

"Yeah, he got riled."

"Oh, my Lord. That's not good!" said Agnes as she began to fan her face with her hand trying to offset the rush of heat she felt creeping up her face.

"Sandra said Jonette told poor ol' Bubba that before she could marry him there was something she had to tell him and she just right then and there, laying in that bed stark-assed nekkid with him, well, she just told Bubba that she used to be a man til she had that, you know, that operation."

"Lord have mercy!" said Agnes as she tried to catch the magazine that fell from her lap.

"I know, I know. I guess Bubba got riled then. First of all, said he puked down the side of the bed. But then something just snapped inside that man. He beat Jonette near to death. He would have finished the job but somebody in the apartment building heard Jonette screaming and called the police. When the police got there, they had to bust in the door and pull Bubba off her. He was hell bent on killing her with his bare hands.

"Lord have mercy on that boy!"

"So, they hauled him off to that there jail. I know his mama's done rolled over in her grave. Like I said, Bubba ain't a bad boy. Not really. That boy's smart as a whip. He used to come in here with his mama. He'd sit right over there in that chair. Always had a comic book with him reading. Shoot his mama taught him to read by the time he was three years old."

Flo looked toward the door as the jingling of the little bell above it alerted her to someone entering her salon.

"Hey, Nadine, honey. Come right on over and sit in that chair. I'll be right with you soon as I get Agnes set."

Flo turned back to the hairdryer, pulling it closer down over Agnes' head.

"Here's your magazine, Agnes. I'll check back with you later."

"Um-hmm." Agnes shook her head and opened her magazine.

Flo scurried over to her next customer.

"How you doing this morning, girl?" Flo asked as she picked out a comb and began combing through Nadine's hair.

"I'm just fine as peach fuzz, Flo. Harvey's coming home tomorrow and I got to get myself all dolled up for him. You know how he likes me to look." Nadine looked at herself in the mirror.

"I know, hon, but I like the way you look today. I don't see how you breathe in those sweaters you wear for Harvey. You want a trim or just style?"

"You better trim it some. You know Harvey. He likes me to show off the girls." Nadine reached down with both hands and lifted her girls to a better position.

"Showing 'em is one thing. Strangling them is another." Flo laughed as she took the scissors from the counter.

"I know. I hate dressing like that. Makes me look like a whore. But Harvey thinks it's sexy and he likes me to look sexy. Says it makes his

37

friends jealous of him." She relaxed back into the chair.

"Nadine, honey, you're just gonna have to grow a back bone one of these days. Now hold still while I trim."

Nadine sat perfectly still. Flo began to snip here and there as the phone on the counter rang.

"Hang on, Nadine, let me get the phone."

"Oh go ahead. I'm not in a hurry."

Flo hurried over to the front counter and picked up the phone receiver.

"Flo's Beauty Boutique."

She stood there in silence listening.

"What? You don't mean to tell me ... That rat-bastard! Okay, okay. Nadine is here with me. You get the others and we can meet here at the shop. Okay, five o'clock. Yeah, we'll think of something."

Flo hung up the phone, took a deep breath and returned to Nadine.

"Listen, Nadine, that was Nancy. There's an emergency meeting of the Sisterhood, here, at five."

"Oh goodness, what's wrong?"

"Never mind now. Nancy will tell us all about it when she gets here."

CHAPTER SIX

The bell over the café door jingled as Spence stepped inside.

"Morning, Spence," said Katy Hughes as she poured a cup of coffee and sat it on the counter in his customary spot. "The usual?"

"Hey, Katy girl, yeah, the usual and how are you this morning?" he replied as he cleaned his boots on the floor mat.

Spence liked the small café with its red checkered table cloths, booths around the outer edge and small tables in the center.

It had a homey feel. It was one of the first places he'd visited when he moved back to Shady Rivers. Its previous owners, John and Billie Kelley, had been good to him and his mother. John was the closest thing he'd had to a real father.

The thing which impressed him most about the café was the Veterans' Table Katy had concocted. He was a Vet himself and he liked the fact she kept the table there.

"Gus, the usual for Spence," she called out. "Well, I'm fine but I had another visit last night."

"What's missing this time?" Spence asked as he threw a leg over the counter stool and sat down.

"Same ol' stuff. Some cans of green beans, eggs, a couple cans of coffee out of the store room, and some slabs of bacon and ham from the cooler. And, as always, a pan of my fried apple pies. The usual stuff."

"Okay, make a list for me. I'll check around and see if anybody saw anything out of the ordinary this time."

Katy reached behind her, took the order Gus sat in the delivery window, and placed it in front of Spence.

"It's sure strange if you ask me," said Katy. "I'm thinking it's somebody a little down on their luck or something."

"Why do you say that?" asked Spence as he took a sip of his coffee.

He had known Katy during the years he and his mom had lived in Shady Rivers. She had always been the bouncy, energetic blonde cheerleader type. Perfect teeth set in a wide mouth, blue eyes and a pixie face. She was kind to a fault. Took in every stray, animal or human, that came along, even ol' Tiny.

Dang bison had just shown up one day and taken over the town. Townsfolk figured he must have come from one of those traveling animal petting zoos. He was rather tame and seemed to love people. Came and went as he chose.

"They only take food, clothes, stuff like that. I mean this donation jar full of money hasn't been touched. And there's plenty of other stuff around here worth a few bucks. Heck, there's even money in the cash register most

40

nights. Never even touched it. It just don't make no sense," replied Katy as she leaned her hip against the counter.

"Well, I haven't seen anybody homeless around here. I'll check around and see if somebody's having it rough these days. Seems ol' man Tuckerman's lost another pair of overalls, too."

"See, just usable stuff. That's all they ever take. I mean this has been going on for a couple of years now. Nobody's ever seen this person. Never seen any tracks or anything. Just don't make no sense at all."

"Yeah, never has made any sense to me either."

Katy turned and grabbed the coffee pot, refilling Spence's cup.

"Enjoy your breakfast now," she said as she headed over to another table of morning patrons.

"You ladies need a refill," asked Katy, as she began to pour coffee into one of the cups.

"I tell you Katy," said Sarah Tuckerman, "this stuff disappearing sure is a puzzlement. I mean what on earth would anybody want with Mel's gosh darned ol' overalls? He wears them until they fall apart. Says they feel better when they's broke in."

"I know what you mean. That's why I think it's somebody who's just down on their luck. You keep an eye out and see if you see anybody wearing those overalls."

"Oh, half the ol' men in town wear overalls. Mel's ain't anything special."

"Well, you might recognize something about them. You just never know," said Katy as

41

she turned around and headed back to the
counter.

CHAPTER SEVEN

"Hey, Nadine, honey," said Flo as she continued sweeping up the hair on the floor from her last customer. "Be a dollbaby and flip that sign over to closed, would you?"

"Oh sure thing," replied Nadine as she closed the Boutique's front door and proceeded to do as she was asked. "Anybody else here yet?"

"Yeah, Dixie and Stella are in the back. Dixie brought some cheesecake and a couple bottles of wine. They're back there getting everything ready."

"Oh my goodness! Must be some serious shit going down if she brought cheesecake."

"I'm afraid it is, honey, some real serious shit is just what it is. You go on back and as soon as Honey closes up shop and gets here I'll lock the doors and we can get started figuring out just what we're gonna to about it, too."

"All right, but I can't stay too long. Harvey should be pulling through town in his truck in a couple of hours. He'll blow his horn and then I gotta run," said Nadine as she headed for the back room.

"Hey girl," said Dixie as she saw Nadine coming through the doorway. "Sit down right over here. I've got you a glass of Moscato right here. We'll dish out the cheesecake as soon as the others get here."

Dixie sat the glass of wine on the small round table in front of Nadine.

"Hey gals," said Nadine as she took a seat where Dixie had indicated.

"Hey, hon," said Stella. "You okay?" she continued as she patted Nadine's hand.

"Sure am, Harvey's due home this evening," she said.

"Oh, hon," said Stella as tears rimmed her eyes.

"Sush, now, Stella," said Dixie. "Give her time to relax a bit. She just needs to unwind for a few minutes until the rest get here."

"Why? What's wrong?" asked Nadine.

"Now, don't you fret about a thing, Nadine, honey, we're going to talk about this little problem and everything will be alright. You'll see," said Dixie as she sat and poured another glass of wine for Stella and herself.

"Hey, how's my favorite gals today?" asked Honey Malone as she waltzed into the room, dressed to the hilt, complete with stilettos and a hat designed for the New York City fashion elite.

"I'm doing just fine," chirped Nadine. "Harvey's due home tonight which means I get laid."

"Well, ain't that just the berries!" said Honey in her sweet Southern drawl.

"Sit down, Hon," said Dixie as Flo pulled out the remaining chair, grabbed a glass and poured herself some wine.

44

"So, now that we're all here, Nadine, honey, I found out something today by accident and I think you should know about it."

"Oh, okay, what is it?"

"Well, see, I was talking to Marge over in T-Town and her sister up in Tennessee had just found out her husband was married to a gal over in Mississippi."

"Oh my gosh, you don't say1" said Nadine. "So we gonna do something about it for her?"

"Naw, honey, that's not all she found out," pipped in Honey. "Seems the no 'count, scum-eatin', egg-suckin' dawg is also married to you."

"W-w-what are you talking about?" asked Nadine as she glanced from Honey to Dixie and back to Honey again.

"Nadine, honey," said Dixie, not only is he married to those two women but there's a third wife in Arkansas. You're number four."

"Four! What do you mean I'm number four?"

"Honey, I know this is difficult but we're going to get you through it. It seems that Harvey has at least four wives we know of and the only problem is, he never divorced any of them, including you."

"Four wives! Harvey has four wives? Are you sure?"

"Yep, said Dixie. I checked it out from the office today. Now listen, I haven't said a word to anybody but the girls here. We need to talk with Dewey over at the office first of all to find out what your legal rights are. You being number four and all."

"Four. Harvey has four wives."

"Give her some more wine, she's still in shock," said Dixie.

Stella picked up the wine bottle and Honey held Nadine's glass while Stella poured.

"Here, drink this Nadine, you'll feel better," said Honey as she handed the glass to Nadine.

Nadine sat there for a moment staring at the glass full of wine before chugging the glass full until it was empty.

"There, that's better," said Nadine. "I'll cut that man's dick off and shove it—"

"Hold onto that thought, hon," said Dixie. "We have to be careful here so the scumbag winds up with nothing when we're through with him."

"But he's due home anytime now," said Nadine, "and the first thing he's going to want to do is strip me nekkid. I can't even stand the thought of him rooting around on top of me!"

"Here's what you do," said Dixie. "You run home and get all the cold and flu medicine you have and put it out on your nightstand. Grab a box of Kleenex and wad them all up and toss them all over the floor. Put some Vick's Salve all over your face, nose, chest. Stink the room up. Mess yourself up from head to toe and get under the bed covers and the minute he comes into the house, start coughing something awful. You've had the flu for two weeks. When he pulls up out here and honks, one of us'll go out and tell him you're sick in bed at home. It won't take him long to figure out he's not going to be getting any nookie from you for another week so he'll come up with some reason to high-tail it out of there and on to the next piece of tail. Can you do that?

"Hell," said Nadine, "I didn't take them acting lessons for nothing. I'll be so close to death's door he won't be able to leave fast enough."

"Okay, sweetie, you go get ready for the acting gig of a lifetime. You'll win an Academy Award for this one. But remember, honey, you've got to act as though you don't know a single thing any different than when he left. Your future is going to depend on it. Okay?" said Dixie.

"I'll be so convincing he won't know a thing."

"Good, go get ready while the girls and I make a plan for plenty of revenge. When we're through with him he'll think twice about getting married again," said Dixie. "Shoot, if you want, we can make him squirm for the next year!"

"Yeah, you go do your best acting ever, Nadine, honey," said Flo, "and don't you worry. He's going to regret the day he came to Shady Rivers and found you."

"Go on before the skunk pulls up. You got to get ready," said Stella.

"You girls are the best friends I could ever have," said Nadine and she hurriedly grabbed her purse and headed out the front door.

CHAPTER EIGHT

It was dusk as Abby stood in the town square gazing up at the mistletoe in the tree. It may have been an old wives' tale, but damn it, it had worked for her grandmother and her mother. She wanted that kind of love. The kind that lasted through the hard times.

She wanted the kind of man who would be there for her. Someone she could share her dreams with, who would be there to encourage her along the way, and celebrate the milestones of life.

She wanted kids. Maybe a whole ball team of kids. She wanted a family to make memories with. Preston never liked Christmas. He refused to put up Christmas decorations and play in the snow.

Damn it, she needed a piece of that mistletoe and she was going to get it. Pulling her coat tighter and tying the hood so it would stay on her head, she took a deep breath and looked upward. All she had to do was keep looking upward and she could make it to that little piece of mistletoe hanging down.

Abby put her foot up on the tree's bottom limb and began to climb upward. Holding her breath, she tried to keep her eyes on the next limb above. She could feel the sweat popping out on her brow.

Keep looking up. You can do this. Just keep looking up.

* * *

Spence finished his meal and watched the lone figure standing in the square looking at the tree. He sipped his coffee waiting.

"You want a slice of pie or anything, Spence?" asked Katy.

"Naw, I have a feeling I'm gonna have to go out there and get somebody out of that dang tree. Damn it! What's wrong with the population around here?"

"How many does that make this time?" asked Katy.

"Well, the one last night was number six and the festival isn't till next week."

"Well, it'll be over then and maybe things will get back to the same ol' same ol'," said Katy. I really do like the festival though, you know. I just love seeing all the stuff people make."

"Yep, we got some right talented people in our neck of the woods, don't we?"

"We sure do. Can't wait to see what ol' Skeeter's done made with his lightnin' bolts."

"He does come up with some nice stuff."

"I swear that boy's been struck by them lightnin' bolts one too many times," she said as she laughed.

"Maybe so. Oops, looks like that one's a climber. Gotta go," said Spence as he stood up and laid a twenty-dollar bill on the counter. "Keep the change, Katy."

"Come on back when you finish. I'll save a piece of my pecan pie for ya."

"Will do," said Spence as he walked out the front door and headed toward the square.

* * *

"I can do this. I can do this," Abby chanted.

Placing her foot on the next limb she lifted herself upward. Her nerves tingled and her breathing grew faster as her fear began to take over. Her palms were moist with sweat.

"I can do this. I can do this."

Her mind flew to the weightless feeling of falling from the tree in her grandmother's back yard. For an instant, it had felt like she was Superman but then came the sudden stop. The breath gushed from her lungs and she felt the pain.

She'd broken her arm and leg. But that pain was nothing compared to the ripping of her heart as she realized the boy she'd had a crush on stood above her, pointing down and laughing loud enough the others heard. Her heart broke into a thousand pieces and she didn't know how to fix it.

He had dared her to climb the tree in the first place. Wanting him to like her, she did what he dared and climbed. After all these years, the memory of his laughter still hurt the most.

"Oh, I can't do this! I just can't do this!" she said as the tears began to wet her eyes.

51

"Hey, you in the tree," called Spence.

"Oh, Spence, thank goodness, you're here. I'm stuck. I'm so scared."

"Abigail Rutledge? What the hell are you doing in that tree?" Spence stood on the ground looking up at Abby.

"I'm stuck, Spence. Hurry, I'm going to fall. I can't do this. I'm so stuck," said Abby as she clung tightly to the tree's trunk.

"Didn't I tell you that mistletoe is not magical. For Pete's sake, you're a grown woman. You should know better."

"Stop fussing at me and get me down," she said as tears began to trickle down her cheeks.

"Oh, hell, don't turn on the faucet. I can't stand that. Hold on, I'm coming up to get you," said Spence as he started up the tree. This time she'd actually made it halfway up the tree.

"Hurry, Spence, I'm so scared."

"Just keep looking up. I'm coming up behind you. No need to be frightened. You're not going to fall. Hold onto the tree and keep looking up."

"Okay, but hurry." Her voice quivered.

Climbing up behind her, Spence pressed his body against hers and placed his hands around each side to grab hold of a limb.

"Okay, now, I've got you. You're safe, now. Take a couple deep breaths. I've got you."

Abby did as she was told and gulped in the air.

Spence could feel her body trembling. She had it bad.

"You're gonna be okay. I've got you. You're not gonna fall. I want you to listen to me.

Concentrate on what I'm telling you, okay? Can you do that?"

"I'm trying, but things are moving. I'm gonna fall."

"Listen to me, Abby. Feel my body behind you. You're not gonna fall. I'd have to fall first and I'm not gonna fall. I've got hold of you. You'll be safe if you just listen to me and do what I tell you to do. I'm not gonna let you fall."

"I'm trying, Spence, I'm trying."

"I know you are. Now listen, I want you to take your right foot and feel for the limb below the one you're standing on."

"I can't. I can't move. I'm going to fall."

"Listen to me, Abby. I'm not going to let you fall. You trust me, don't you?"

"I-I—"

Spence pressed his cheek against the side of her face, close to her ear.

"Remember all those nights we had wild monkey sex you told me about?"

"We did not!"

"Move your foot, Abby. Yeah, we were having wild sex in your bedroom. You probably tore my shirt off, I'll bet," he said.

Keeping her mind off what she was doing wasn't going to be easy since it was keeping his mind on what he'd like to be doing. Pressed up against her, like that, he could smell the shampoo in her hair. Smelled like Johnson's Baby Shampoo and her hair felt so silky soft.

"Now move your foot down. I've got you. What'd you do after you took off my shirt? Maybe I unbuttoned your blouse. I'll bet I did it really slow. Button by button. Bet I made you beg me to hurry. Is that what happened, Abby?"

53

"Yes, no, I mean—"

"Move your other foot down. What do you mean, Abby? Tell me what we did in your fantasy." Spence felt his erection pressing against Abby's cute butt.

"I can't."

"Yes, you can. Move your other foot. We're almost down, just keep looking up. Tell me about your fantasy. Did you unzip my pants?" *I hope you did and if we don't get down from here soon I'm going to have to strip you naked right here.*

"Are we down yet?"

"Almost. You're doing just fine. A couple more steps is all it takes. Keep looking up," he said. "Breathe."

"I'm so scared," she said as she moved her foot down another step.

"You're doing just fine. We're having sex, remember. Just like you want it. I'm kissing you all over," he said as his lips touched the side of her neck.

"Spence, I—"

"It's okay, Abby, don't think. Just feel. Feel my lips against your skin," he said as he guided her down another limb.

"That feels so good," said Abby as her mind momentarily grasped the sensation he was causing. A warm feeling traveled from her neck straight down to her core. She wanted more.

"Yeah, it feels nice doesn't it. You smell good." He nipped at her earlobe with his teeth.

Abby groaned as she felt her nipples harden.

"One more time. Move your right foot down and you'll feel the ground. Go ahead. Move it. I've got you," said Spence.

"Are we down yet?" asked Abby.

"Almost."

With one last step, Abby stood with both feet on the ground at the bottom of the tree.

"See, now, that wasn't so hard, was it?" He stood still pressing her against the tree. Abby waited for him to release her and move away. His lips grazed her neck. She shuddered with his touch. Her breathing came in quick gulps as she tried to flush the thoughts of his erection pressed hard against her out of her mind. It felt so good. She would definitely be having those fantasies about him tonight. That was for sure.

CHAPTER NINE

"Spence," said Abby.

"Yeah."

"You can let me go now. I think I'm okay."

"Oh, yeah," he said as he stepped backward. He had to get his thoughts under control and stop his body's reaction to her. He turned her around to face him. "What the hell were you doing up there?"

"I know, I know. I'm not supposed to be up there but—"

"No. There are no buts. Stay out of that damn tree. That mistletoe is not magical. You're a grown woman. A judge no less and you, of all people, should know there is no such thing as magic."

"I know, but—"

"No. No buts. If I catch you in that tree again, I'll have to give you a ticket. You'll have to appear in court and that won't look good on Your Honor's record, now would it?" he said as he placed his arm around her shoulders. "Now where's your car?"

"At my house. I walked this afternoon. It was still daylight and I walked to the bakery for a piece of Mrs. Becky's cheesecake. Figured I'd walk it off going back home. But, then I saw the tree."

"And you thought you'd just climb it off instead. What the hell is wrong with you? You could have gotten hurt."

"Well, I just have to have a piece of that mistletoe."

"Listen," said Spence as he stopped and turned her to face him. "That mistletoe has nothing to do with you and what's his name. He's not even here. So see, even if you did manage to climb up there and get a piece of mistletoe, he wouldn't be the first person you see."

"But—"

"No. I told you already, no buts. You're at a greater risk of getting hurt climbing up there simply because of your fear of heights. You freeze up. If I hadn't been watching, you could have been stuck up there all night and in addition to that you could have gotten hypothermia. I mean it's downright cold out here."

"I know," she said as she glanced away.

"Listen, Abby," he said as he turned her cheek to face him. "You have to promise me you won't try this again. I don't want to see you hurt. And, really, there is no such thing as magical mistletoe. You have to know that."

"I know I shouldn't climb up there with my fear of heights but I just really need to know."

"You'll just have to find a different way to know. You're not climbing that tree. Now come on and I'll take you home," he said as he took her by the hand and started walking across the square toward his own truck.

"Seems like you're always rescuing me."

"Just consider me a knight in shining armor who rescues damsels in distress."

"Well, you've certainly rescued me enough times. I'll try to stay out of the tree."

"I'd appreciate it if you'd do more than try. Just stay out of the damned tree. Come on, my truck's over right over there."

* * *

Pulling into Abby's driveway, Spence turned off the ignition, jumped out of the truck and walked around to open her door.

"You don't have to see me to the door. I can find my way."

"I always make sure damsels in distress make it home safely," he said as he helped her down. Placing her arm into the crook of his, he headed toward the front porch. "Besides, I don't get to escort a Judge home very often." He smiled at her.

Stepping up on the porch, Abby pulled her housekey from her coat pocket and opened the door. For a moment, she hesitated.

"Would you like to come in for a cup of coffee?" she asked as she turned to face him.

"I'd really like to but I'm on duty until ten."

"Well, if the lights are on, coffee's hot."

"Thanks, I just may take you up on that." Spence smiled. "After all, you might need more ideas for that wild monkey sex we been having."

"Now, see, I can't live here. You would never, ever let me forget that." Abby said as she reached to open the door.

"Probably not," Spence said as he leaned over and kissed her cheek. "But, we can make it

59

true any time you like." Spence laughed as he turned and stepped off the porch and headed back to his truck.

A smile crept across Abby's face as she turned and walked inside closing the door behind her.

* * *

Spence parked in front of Katy's Kitchen, glancing at the tree in the square across the street. Maybe they should just hire someone to cut that damnable mistletoe out of the tree before Christmas ever got there. Then, maybe the women folk would stop all this nonsense.

Grown people believing in magic. Nonsense. Pure and simple nonsense. But then, it did draw tourists to the town and that really wasn't all bad.

Spence glanced at his watch. Mike South would be there soon to take over.

Walking into the café, Spence nodded at Katy as she looked up from wiping down the counter.

"Hey, Spence. Who'd you pull out of the tree this time?"

"Abby Rutledge. Damn woman's afraid of heights, too."

"Ethel's granddaughter? When'd she get back in town?"

"Few days ago," said Spence as he sat on the stool in front of the counter.

"What the hell's she doing climbing that stupid tree?" That girl's been afraid of heights ever since she fell out of one," Katy said as she

60

poured a cup of coffee and sat it in front of Spence.

"Trying to get a piece of that mistletoe like every other person within fifty miles. She fell out of a tree?" he asked, taking a sip of coffee.

"Yeah, as a kid. If I remember right, she broke her arm and a leg, too, I think."

"When was that?"

"Let's see. That was the same year her mom and dad were killed in that car accident. People were stopping by her grandma's house. You know, dropping off casseroles and stuff like that. A bunch of us kids were out back playing. Abby'd climbed up that big ol' sequoia tree in the back yard. Fell out of the darn thing and her grandma and, I think it was Elmer Shelton and his wife, who took her over to the hospital in Tuscaloosa."

"Well, if she don't stop trying to climb this one she's gonna break something else," said Spence, as he sat his coffee cup back down on the counter.

"I just don't understand people sometimes," said Katy as she continued her cleaning.

"Guess it just takes all kinds to make a world," replied Spence.

"Well now, you take that person who's been stealing stuff. I mean, why not ask people for it?"

"Well, if they're down on their luck, they may be too embarrassed to ask," said Spence as he took a sip of his coffee.

"Hadn't thought of that. Hey, maybe I'll leave them a note and ask if there's something they really need. I could set up a box and just leave whatever they needed in it. Then they wouldn't be stealing it. That might make 'em feel better about themselves."

"That's a good idea. If there's kids involved they could leave sizes for shoes and stuff and maybe somebody with kids who've outgrown their sizes would drop it off."

"That's just perfect. I'll make up a flyer telling people what we're gonna do and I'll leave a note out every night with my fried apple pies. They always take some of my pies so they'll be sure to see the note and they'll see we want to help."

"I think that'll be perfect."

"Great. I'll have Gus get one of those big boxes from the back room and I'll get it set up tonight."

"Looks, like you got a visitor there," said Spence as he nodded toward the side window where Tiny stood licking at the glass.

"I think he eats more of my fried apple pies than anybody in town," Katy laughed as she slid the glass door open and picked up a pie before heading to the window.

"Well, hello there big feller," she cooed, "Stopping by for one last treat before heading home, are ya? Well, give mama a kiss first." Katy leaned out the window letting the bison lick the side of her face. "That's mama's good boy," she said as she scratched behind his ears while he gently took the offered pie, chomped a few times, turned and headed down the street continuing his nightly round. "I'm gonna miss that ol' guy if he ever decides to leave," she said turning back to Spence.

"With you feeding him apple pies he ain't going nowhere. And if you ever decide to leave, you'll have to take him with you or he'll just grieve himself to death."

"Guess we don't have to worry about that then. Now where were we?"

"You were gonna fix a donation box."

"Oh, yeah."

"I'll donate some stuff. Was gonna clean out my closet anyway," said Spence as he stood up, tossed a couple dollars on the counter and started toward the door. "You be sure Gus walks you home. Too many visitors coming through town these days."

"Oh, you know, Gus, ever since he started working here, he don't let me out of his sight. Guess he wants to be sure nothing happens to me or he'd be out of a job."

"You ever think there might be another reason?" said Spence as he walked out closing the door behind him.

"Now what the hell did he mean by that?" said Katy as she stuck her pencil in its place behind her right ear.

CHAPTER TEN

Walking around the town square, Spence stopped at each business, turning the doorknobs to make sure they were locked up tight. After finishing up with the front doors, he stepped around to the back of his office building and started his round of checking the back doors.

Satisfying himself that all was safe and secure for the moment, he made his way back to his office and put on a pot of coffee. He had a little bit of paperwork to take care of before Mike came in.

He really appreciated the help the police academy in Tuscaloosa sent him during the festival. Shady Rivers could barely afford to pay Spence himself so the academy sent trainees out for a couple of weeks. It was good practical experience for the trainees plus it helped Spence with the crazies during festival time. He figured it was a win-win situation for both.

Spence finished his paperwork just minutes before Mike arrived. Grabbing his jacket, he headed to his truck and home. Passing Abby's house, he noticed her light was still on as he pulled into his own drive. Turning off the truck's motor, he sat there staring at her house.

The house had sat empty since Mrs. Ruthledge's death six months ago. It had never bothered him until now. Now it held something he *wanted* and he hadn't felt this much *want* in quite some time. He wanted that woman, although the why of wanting this particular woman was beyond him.

She'd climbed right into his life that first night and he'd have a heck of a time getting her out again. But then he wasn't sure he wanted her out.

This female was going to be his curse. She was so unlike him. Sentimental, stubborn, and even believed in ol' wives' tales of all things.

Women were just that way and he'd managed to steer clear of them for the most part.

Maybe this one was just an itch that definitely needed to be scratched.

Spence cranked his truck, backed out of his drive and drove the short distance to Abby's. Turning off his truck, he sat for a moment still thinking about the woman inside the house. *Turn around ol' man. There's nothing there for you.* He knew that argument all too well. He'd already had it the few time he'd seen her.

Then he heard his mother's voice. Just a whisper. *It's magical.* He knew better. There was no such thing. How many times had he and his mother stood in front of that stupid tree? No, there was no such thing as magic.

But, for some reason, he just couldn't ignore this itch. This one was an itch that definitely needed a good scratching.

Opening his truck door, he stepped outside. The night air was crisp and clear. It smelled of the evergreen trees like the ones he and his mom planted when his stepdad had moved them there years ago. Walking onto Abby's porch, he knocked on her door.

He could hear her coming. All of a sudden, he felt like a teenage boy on his first date. His nerves decided to play havoc with the rest of his body and he could feel the sweat starting between his shoulder blades.

The door opened and Spence's heart skipped a beat.

"God, you're beautiful," he blurted out before he could stop himself.

"Thank you. I'm going to assume you didn't stop by just to tell me that," replied Abby with a laugh.

"I saw your light on."

"Would you like to come in for that cup of coffee?" Abby stepped back to allow room for Spence to enter.

"A cup of coffee sounds good." Spence stepped inside, quickly glancing around. "I don't ever remember being inside your grandma's house before."

"You know, it's funny but I don't remember you as a kid," said Abby as she led the way to the kitchen.

"Kept to myself, I reckon. Don't remember a lot of the kids around here myself. Besides, we only lived here a few years before we moved. My mom had this thing about basements. She hated the one in that house. Wouldn't go down there. Even nailed the door shut. Guess she felt about basements like some women feel about spiders and snakes."

Abby reached into the cabinet and pulled out two coffee mugs.

"You take anything in yours," she asked.

"Nope. I like my coffee strong and black."

"Me, too. I remember hearing my grandmother say, 'don't want no watered-down coffee' when people would ask her if she wanted sugar and cream. She used to give me sips of it from a spoon. Gosh, but those are good memories." Abby smiled.

"What kind of memories are you making now," asked Spence looking over the rim of his cup as he took a sip of the hot liquid.

"You ask hard questions," she replied.

"Guess they could be if you don't know the answer," said Spence as he sat the mug down on the counter. "This boyfriend of yours, he helping you make good memories?" Spence continued as he reached out and pushed a tendril of flame red hair from Abby's face.

Abby momentarily leaned into his hand and closed her eyes. Realizing what she was doing, she quickly opened them and met Spence's gaze. She stared at him for moment. This was dangerous ground she was treading on and she knew it. He was a nice, caring person.

Running in the opposite direction was what she should be doing, yet there was something about him that made her want to get to know him better. Maybe if she just got to know him a little bit, she'd never have to see him enough to form any kind of attachment to him. He'd just be somebody to talk with for a few days. Then, she'd be gone and she could go back to her normal life. Besides she needed a little bit of fun for a change. She'd worked long, hard hours getting her grandmother's house ready to sell like Preston wanted. Now, while there was someone nice around, maybe she could take advantage of the situation and just enjoy herself before settling down for good.

Only a moment passed before he leaned in and his lips touched hers. Soft and sensual at first, turned into hot and torrid in a matter of seconds.

CHAPTER ELEVEN

"Abby, I—"

Reaching up, she placed her finger on his lips. She wanted this. It seemed as though she'd known him all her life and had been waiting for this very moment.

"Shhh," she said, "we've already done this every night in my dreams, remember?"

He kissed her lips and moved his hand up underneath her sweater cupping her breast. His thumb traced her hardening nipple. Shoving her sweater up, his mouth kissed her breast through her bra. Reaching around behind her, he unsnapped her bra freeing the mounds of soft flesh he found there. He felt her response to his touch.

She felt warm and soft. He needed to lose himself inside her. Her fragrance assaulted his senses.

Spence picked her up and turned.

"Bedroom?"

"That way," she said nodding.

Moments later, Spence laid her on the bed and quickly unbuttoned her sweater, tossing it aside along with her bra. His mouth found her nipple and he flicked it with his tongue eliciting moans of pleasure from her. Unzipping her jeans, he slid them and her panties down her legs and tossed them aside. He wanted to feel his skin against hers. Grabbing the opening of his shirt, he popped the buttons, ripping it off. Unzipping his jeans, he quickly discarded them.

He left a trail of kisses from her nipple up to her lips where he began a slow exploration of her sensuous mouth. Feeling her respond, his own reactions heated more. His body covered hers as she spread her legs to allow him access. His fogged brain allowed his senses to run on autopilot. He held his weight above her and thrust his hardness into her moist, warm center. She gasped and pulled him tighter. He felt her hands digging at his back with each heated thrust. His movements became fast and furious.

All he could think about was the feeling of pleasure she was giving him. With each thrust he wanted to plunge deeper into her core. He kissed her neck spurring her reactions to him. He felt her movements matching his as he plunged into her and knew she was getting close to her own release. He thrust into her hard and with one hand took her nipple, pulling at it with his thumb and forefinger.

Her movements quickened; her breathing already hard and irregular. She clawed at his back begging him for more. With each word she uttered he gave her more of himself. He wanted her pleasure to increase; he wanted the pleasure she was allowing him to be as good for her as it was for him.

He felt her sex pulling at him and felt her body stiffen as her climax released her pleasure. His own release of hot liquid exploded as he shoved his throbbing member deep inside her. As his movements slowed, he showered kisses along her neck. He felt her relax. After a few moments, he rolled off her and drew her into his body to keep her warm. Stroking her cheek, he whispered a thank you in her ear.

"That was wonderful," she said. "I could get use to this if it was always this good."

"Me, too," he whispered as he held her close.

They lay snuggled in each other's arms until sleep overtook them both.

Spence awoke to the woman lying beside him pushing her warm butt against him. The hard-on she was causing needed some relief and obviously she did, too. His mind was still clouded from sleep but from the evidence on display, his libido wasn't. Reaching over, he kissed her softly on her neck.

Turning toward him, she moaned in approval. He kissed her lips and moved his hand up cupping her breast, his thumb tracing her hardening nipple. She responded to his touch.

Kisses trailed upon kisses with bodies entwined until they could not tell where one started and the other stopped.

Abby's hands roamed Spence's shaved head as he left a trail of tingling flesh as he kissed his way to her lower region. She moaned with her pleasure. Grabbing his ears gently, she pulled him back up to kiss her hot mouth.

"Now, Spence, now," she begged him as she spread her legs waiting for his entrance to her core.

Spence did not make her wait long for her climax. He thrust his manhood into her soft warm folds of female flesh time and again as fast and furious as he could give it to her and her climax rose higher with each thrust, until she finally headed over the precipice and down the other side calling out his name.

Moments later, they lay snuggled against each other's exhausted body.

"I could get used to getting woke up for middle of the night sex," she whispered.

"Me, too," he whispered back as he held her close while she drifted back to sleep. When he felt her breathing relax into a steady rhythm, he allowed himself to fall back asleep.

CHAPTER TWELVE

The ladies of the Sisterhood sat around the little round table in the back of Flo's Beauty Boutique. They had all arrived promptly at seven that morning. Flo had the coffee hot and black. She knew they'd need it for what they were planning.

"Okay," said Dixie, "here's what I found out. Mr. Howe said that since Harvey had never divorced his first wife, she was the one who would be entitled to whatever the scumbag has if they divorce. Plus, since he was never divorced in the first place, you aren't legally married to him."

"You mean all this time I've been living with Harvey we ain't been married?"

"No hon, you haven't," said Dixie as she patted Nadine's hand.

"Lord have mercy! My mama's done rolled over in her grave. Me living in sin like that. Lord Jesus help me!" More tears poured down Nadine's puffy face.

"Don't you worry yourself none. Mr. Howe said he could do an annulment for you and that would take care of it. But, now, in the meantime, before Harvey finds out anything is up, Nadine, honey, you need to go to the bank and close out the joint bank account you have. Take it all. Every last cent and put it in a bank account with just your name on it. Okay?"

"Okay. Close joint account and open one in my name," said Nadine as she scribbled on her notepad.

"Is the house in both your names?" asked Honey.

"No, thank goodness. It was mine before we married. Inherited it after mom and dad passed away."

"Then that's good," said Dixie.

"How about your convertible?" asked Stella.

"That was a present from Harvey. Only has my name on it."

"Good. Anything you can think of that has his name attached to it?" asked Dixie.

"I have one credit card with his name on it. He gave that to me in case of an emergency or something."

"Well, this is an emergency. Go out and stock up your freezer, repair anything that needs to be repaired. That type of thing. Max it out with whatever you're going to need to get by for the next year. He owes you that much."

"Oh goodness, I've been doing laundry by hand and hanging it out to dry 'cause Harvey said we didn't have enough for a new washer and dryer just yet."

"That pig!" said Honey. "Wonder if his other wives had washers and dryers."

"Well, I don't know about them but I'm fixin' to have me a new set. Anybody wanna go shopping this afternoon?" said Nadine smiling through her tears.

"That's the spirit, Nadine. It's time this piece of trash realized just who he messed with," said Stella. "I got time this afternoon. I have to go drop off some paperwork for the office over at the Tuscaloosa courthouse. Won't take but a minute, then we can spend the rest of the afternoon doing a little light shopping." Stella laughed.

"Okay, I'll get ready and pick you up at the office around eleven. Is that okay?" asked Nadine.

"Sure. That'll just be perfect."

"Okay," said Dixie. "You've got your work cut out for you then, Nadine. So you get all that taken care of today and then we'll go on to the next round after that. We've only got about thirty days before all these charges start showing up on Harvey's credit card bills and he starts figuring out something's wrong so we gotta work fast."

CHAPTER THIRTEEN

The morning sun streamed through Abby's bedroom window warming her face. She slowly became aware of morning and a warm body lying next to her. Snuggling closer, a masculine scent flooded her senses and her hand, splayed across his lower abdomen, tangled with coarse hair. She felt his hardness nudging at the back of her hand.

She lay perfectly still as the memory of Spence slipped quietly into her brain. It was a good memory.

"Morning Sunshine," said Spence as he rolled toward Abby.

"Is it morning already?" she asked as she felt his hardness nudging at her.

"That it is, sweetheart, and I'm afraid I'm already late for work."

"Oh my goodness, what time is it?" said Abby as she sat up in bed.

"It's nine already."

"I'm so sorry. I haven't slept this late in years. I'll go make some coffee and you can take a shower before you go, if you like."

"I have a better idea," said Spence with a grin on his face, as he pulled her back down beside him.

"We could save on water. You know conservation and all that stuff. I could wash your back and you could wash mine," he said as he lowered his lips onto hers.

"Mmmmmmmmmmmm," said Abby as her lips lingered on his.

Pulling away, Spence crawled out of bed and pulled Abby up and rested her across his shoulders as he padded toward the bathroom. Once inside, he let her down gently into the shower and turned on the water, and stepped in beside her.

Taking the scrubbie from its place, he lathered it with soap and began to wash her back. Watching as the soap bubbles caressed her wet skin, he rubbed her shoulders, before letting his washing motions travel down between her shoulder blades, watching as the soap cascaded down her back.

She was definitely enjoying what he was doing. Her eyes closed and her body moved underneath each caress. She seemed to be relaxing with the combination of hot water and his massage. The soap scented her body a nice fragrance of honeysuckle.

He moved his hands lower, caressing her buttocks before trailing back up and around her waist. Her breathing was more rapid and she moaned softly. She seemed to be lost in the pleasure he was creating for her and he let his hands continue their massaging effects upwards to her breast. Abby moaned as he kissed her neck and trailed kisses across her shoulders. Her pleasure seemingly increasing dramatically with each touch. He continued until her knees buckled under her.

80

Lifting her to his waist, she locked her legs around him and he backed her into the shower wall. His hard shaft found the entrance it desired and slowly he pushed his way inside. She felt wonderful. Nothing he'd had before felt quite like this woman. She was warm, moist and tight around his penis. He could feel the muscles of her sex pulling him in. He stood there for a moment savoring the pleasure of her. Her luscious breasts pushed against his chest.

Spence felt his cock pulse inside her and he couldn't hold himself still any longer. She could give him the release he craved. He kissed her neck and gently rubbed her breast with his hand. Thrusting himself inside her, he pushed again and again into her warm center, his climax building. He didn't know how much longer he could hold off, but he was determined to take her to her own heights of satisfaction.

He felt her body stiffen and she began clawing at his back as though she were trying to draw her climax all the way through him. He shoved into her again and let his climax take him with her as they fell over the edge of passion. His tongue danced inside her mouth as he kissed her again and again, wanting to taste every inch of her.

"Oh, Spence, that was so wonderful," she whispered when he finally ended the kiss.

"I thought so, too," he said as he held her close. "Now, I do hate to kiss and run but my deputy is gonna be mighty pissed at me already."

"No, you go, I understand. Besides, I've got plenty of work to do around here."

"Can I take you to dinner tonight?" Spence asked as he grabbed a towel and stepped from the shower.

"You could, but how about if I make you dinner to pay you back for the other night?" said Abby as she grabbed her own towel.

"I'd like that, but you don't have to pay me back," he said.

"Okay, we'll just consider it dinner between friends. What time do you get off work?" Abby asked as she wrapped the towel around her and tucked it in front.

"If all goes well, I should be off at six today."

"Great, how about seven then?"

"Seven it is. Can I bring anything?" he asked as he headed for the bedroom and his clothes.

"Nope. Just bring yourself. You'll be working all day and I won't, so I'll take care of everything."

Spence quickly dressed and headed to the front door. "See you tonight then," he said as he took her in his arms and kissed her lips. "And if I keep this up any longer, I'm going to have to take that towel off you and I'll have Mike looking for me."

"Well, I don't want to be arrested for interfering with police duties, so you'd best be on your way," she said as she shoved him out the door.

* * *

After dressing in a fresh pair of jeans and sweatshirt, Abby busied herself with going through the rest of her grandmother's things to try and decide what to do with it all.

There were so many memories in this old house. A plate of her grandmother's warm sugar cookies and a cold glass of milk sitting on the table

82

waiting for her when she got off the bus from school; lying in bed at night while her grandmother read from *Laura Ingalls Wilder* or a *Nancy Drew* book, even dancing around the kitchen as her grandmother taught her how to dance for her first boy/girl dance. Those were good memories. Those were memories she would cherish.

Climbing the stairs to the attic, she quietly opened the old door. A few cobwebs hung here and there, and a dust film covered most everything. Abby carefully stepped among the things her grandmother had stored there long ago. The attic was quiet with an almost reverent hush. It felt as though all her ancestors were there, watching, waiting.

An old rocking chair sat beside the attic window. Abby sat down and opened the big trunk which sat beside it. Lying on top of the trunk's contents, she saw her favorite bear. Bear, the teddy bear had been with her since her parents died in a car accident when she was four years old.

Abby took out the photo album, rubbing her hand across it's worn leather cover. She and her grandmother had spent hours putting new photos in and reminiscing over the old ones.

Sometimes they had cried together over the photos of her mom and dad, while other days brought laughter at all the fun they'd had. It had been hard for Abby to remember her mom and dad at times, but grandmother had told her the stories until it was almost as though she remembered the details herself.

It was noon by the time she'd finished looking through the album and reminiscing. Placing the album back in its resting place, she picked up Bear and headed back down the stairs, closing the attic door behind her. Preston would just have to understand. She could not sell this house. It was the last connection she had with her parents and she just could not bear to let it go. At least not yet.

* * *

Spence stepped onto Abby's porch promptly at seven. He thought about just opening the door and yelling "Honey, I'm home!" but thought better of it and rang the doorbell instead. There was just something about this woman that tugged at him. Something deep in the recesses of his soul but he couldn't quite bring it to the surface.

He felt like a school boy on his first date. He'd picked up a bouquet of carnations with a few roses tucked in here and there, along with a bottle of *Stella Rosa* semi-sweet wine, so he wasn't empty handed. He shifted his weight from one foot to the other and felt the heat around his shirt collar.

If he wasn't careful, this lady would have him jumping through hoops in no time at all. That was something he wanted to avoid. Love didn't last. Even his own mom hadn't found happiness by being married to his stepdad. After all these years, Spence could still hear her screams. He wouldn't think of it now.

Abby opened the door, and Spence saw the look of delight cross her face as she saw the flowers.

"Oh, my goodness, flowers! And they're so beautiful," she said as she stepped back allowing him to enter.

"And their beauty fails in comparison to you," said Spence as he handed them to her.

"Thank you," said Abby, "that's the nicest thing anyone's said to me in ages." She took the flowers and stood on tiptoes as she placed a quick kiss on Spence's cheek.

"You should hear compliments on a daily basis," said Spence, "you deserve them."

"I'm not so sure about that but I do thank you and thank you for these beautiful flowers. Come on into the kitchen while I put them in some water."

Spence followed Abby watching her backside as he went. *Nice view.*

"Have a seat there at the bar. Dinner's almost ready and it'll just take me a minute to get these in a vase," she said as she grabbed a vase from the cupboard underneath the sink, filled it with water and sat it next to the phone on the breakfast bar.

"So how was your day?"

"Nostalgic, I guess."

Abby sat a salad on the counter, turned and dished up two plates of baked lasagna along with garlic bread. She sat one plate in front of Spence and the other for herself. Turning, she grabbed two glasses of sweet tea from the fridge before sitting down at the bar across from Spence.

"And what brought on this nostalgia?" asked Spence, watching as Abby dropped her gaze to the food on her plate. He was already a gonner for this woman and he knew it.

"Oh, I was just trying to decide on things in the house to keep and things to get rid of. Made the mistake this morning of starting with the things stored in the attic. There was a chest of photos and things and I sat up there just going through it. Found some things my grandmother kept that I'd forgotten about," she said as she sipped her tea.

"Like what?" asked Spence.

"Like my teddy bear," said Abby. "I got it when I fell out of a tree years ago."

"So, you were a tree climber back then, too, huh?"

"Oh yeah, big time," laughed Abby as she took a bite of her lasagna.

"And did you get stuck back then, too?"

"I'd say so. Guess I was just born with this fear of heights. The last tree I tried to climb was at my old home with my mom and dad. It was a big one in the backyard. I fell and broke a few bones. Haven't tried to climb anything since, well, except for the mistletoe tree."

"So why were you trying to climb that tree?"

"Oh, just trying to fit in with the rest of the kids, I guess."

"Don't tell me someone as pretty as you didn't fit in."

"Well, when you're afraid of heights and all the other kids are climbing up on the slide and sliding down and you're standing on the sideline watching, you feel like you don't fit in."

"Guess I hadn't thought about like that," said Spence as he picked up his glass of tea and took a drink.

"Any way, there was this boy I liked. But he was always paying attention to all the other girls and never me. At least that's how it felt to me. He dared me to climb the tree."

"Did he know you were afraid of heights?"

"Oh, yeah, that's why he did it."

"And you fell?"

"Yep. He and the others just stood there laughing. I think the laughter hurt worse than the broken bones."

"He sounds like your typical bully to me."

"He was. But I guess it was what he grew up with. He wound up in prison by the time he was eighteen."

"That's too bad. Did the other kids treat you better after that?"

"No, not really. I kind of kept to myself after that. You know, I think a lot of kids don't think about the kid on the sideline."

"You just may be onto something there," said Spence.

"How about more lasagna?"

"Oh my goodness, woman, if I eat any more I won't be able to get up off this stool," said Spence with a laugh. "How about if you just take your pretty little self, right on into that living room and have a seat. I'll clean up the kitchen and join you as soon as I'm finished."

"Well, that does sound like a very tempting offer, but if we both clean that'll get us both into the living room much faster, don't you think?" said Abby with a smile on her face.

"Now, that's even a more tempting offer," said Spence as he squiggled his eyebrows in Grouch Marx style.

Abby laughed as she stood and gathered her plate, silverware and glass as she headed for the dishwasher.

Spence fell in line behind her watching her hips sway in perfectly fluid motion.

Minutes later, walking into the living room with a bottle of wine and two glasses, Spence gazed fleetingly around the room but stopped short when he saw the teddy bear sitting on one end of the mantel. There was something familiar, yet he couldn't quite place it. It was there, in the cobwebs of his mind, but seemingly just out of reach. He glanced back at Abby.

"Come, sit with me awhile. I know you'll have to guard the tree again. But look at it this way. As long as you're here with me, I'm not stuck in it." Abby laughed.

"Well, that is a plus," said Spence as he handed Abby the two glasses and opened the bottle of wine before he sat down close to her and put his arm behind her, resting it on the couch. He poured the two glasses and set the bottle on the end table.

Taking the glass of wine Abby held for him, Spence glanced back up at the bear. What was it about that darn bear. If he could just dig it up from the recesses of his mind.

"Did you make any decisions about this beautiful old house?" asked Spence.

"No, not really. I just need to stop thinking and let Preston take care of it. He's good with figures and says, in the long run, we'd be better without it."

"But will YOU be better without it?" Spence asked as he gently turned her face toward him. "I'm usually not one to meddle, but it seems to me, since this is your house, you should be the one to decide if you want to keep it or not. And it's not about the money. It's about the memories, the people who lived here, the little girl who grew up here. It's about are you ready to let go and move on or is this a part of you you're not ready to let go of yet."

"Oh, I don't know. I'm just confused and making all these decisions right now is hard. Can we talk about something else?"

"Sure," said Spence as he relaxed back sipping his wine. "Is that the bear you were talking about earlier?" said Spence as he pointed at it with his wine glass.

"Yes, that's Bear."

"Bear. Now that's an original name for a bear."

"Don't blame me. I was only four years old when I got him. What do you expect from a four-year-old?"

"I don't know. Maybe Goldilocks or something." Spence grinned at her.

"Oh you," said Abby as she playfully punched him in the shoulder.

"Your grandmother get him for you?"

"No, he was given to me by someone I didn't know. A little boy. Years ago.

"Ah, an admirer. And at such an early age."

"No. Actually, it was the day I fell out of the tree. My grandmother had to take me to the hospital to set the fractures. I don't remember a whole lot of what went on."

"That's good. I guess Mother Nature has a way of letting us forget the bad parts of life."

"She does let us remember the good parts though because I remember, as we were leaving the hospital, the nurse was pushing me in a wheelchair, grandma was on the other side and I'd been crying quite a bit. Someone my grandmother knew was walking toward us and she had her little boy with her. Apparently, she'd heard and had come to the hospital to be with my grandma in case she needed anything."

"That was thoughtful of her."

"It's funny. None of the other people we knew came to the hospital. I thought about it later. How nice and kind this woman was to show up. Anyway, she had brought her son and he was carrying this teddy bear. He handed it to me and told me not to cry anymore because Bear was there. And that Bear had courage and he would be a good friend and I could tell him anything."

"Bear. I'll be damned! That's Bear."

"Yep, that's Bear."

"Yeah, that's what I mean," said Spence as he jumped up and hurried over to the bear. "This bear is Bear. What happened to the Boy Scout pin he wore on his vest?"

Abby sat there for a minute trying to grasp what Spence was trying to say. Then it hit her. All the air left her lungs at once. Her heartbeat swooshed inside her ears and she could feel the blood pounding around her temples. She opened her mouth to speak but words wouldn't come out.

"You okay?" asked Spence as he noticed the color drain from Abby's face.

Abby nodded yes, then no, and then yes again. When she was able to speak again, the words rushed out.

"It was you," she whispered. "You were the little boy who gave me Bear?"

Spence rushed back over to Abby.

"I'm sorry. I never connected it together until you said the thing about him having courage. I mean, that little banged up girl and you. I mean, that was so many years ago. But, Bear. Bear was a favorite of mine."

"Mine, too."

"See, he was given to me by someone I really don't remember. My dad. My real dad, not my stepdad. My dad told me bears were born with plenty of courage. They lived in the woods, hunted and fished for their food, protected their young and all sorts of stuff. And that anytime I needed a little dab of courage I should just hold Bear close and he'd share his courage with me. So, I took him places with me when I was unsure. You know, places I'd never been before and especially to doctors' offices and such. I earned that Boy Scout badge for courage. Thought Bear deserved it more than I did, so I pinned it on him."

"But you gave him to me. Why?"

"Because at that moment, you needed him more than I did."

"But to give up something that meant a great deal to you. And you gave him to someone you didn't even know."

"Well, all I knew was that you were hurting. I could see the fright in your eyes. I guess I just knew how that felt and I didn't want you to feel that way. Guess I was just practicing my courage."

"That Bear is the most precious thing I own. But he belongs to you. You should take him home with you."

"No, you keep him. I still see some fright in those pretty green eyes of yours," he said as he leaned over and kissed her forehead. "As a matter of fact, I think you may need him more now than that little four-year-old girl did." He pulled her closer and gently settled her head against his chest.

"Some days I feel like that little four-year-old girl." She curled her legs up beside her, resting

91

against Spence's body. She felt safe wrapped in the cocoon of his arms.

"Did you ever think that maybe you feel that way because you're trying to live up to someone else's expectations of you instead of your own?" He kissed the top of her head softly.

"I guess I have always tried to be the person everyone wants me to be. I mean, that's just what people do. You try to please everybody. I guess it's just that some people want more than I can give."

"You know the one thing I'd like you to be?"

"See, even you want me to be your kind of person," said Abby as she looked up at him.

"The only kind of person I want you to be is yourself. Just relax, let go and be yourself for a change. You might find you like it." Spence smiled and moved his lips a whisper length from hers. "Take charge, Abby. Let your own wants take over for a change. Take what Abby wants."

Abby closed the distance as she devoured his lips. She needed this man. She wanted this man. He was so different from every man she'd ever known. He was so kind, loving and caring. He made her heart sing and her soul rejoice. In his arms, she was happy. She was safe. She felt loved. *Oh my God, I've fallen in love.*

The truth hit her like a ton of bricks, but she only wanted more. She needed him more than she needed any man in her life. He had told her to take what she wanted, and she wanted him now.

Abby moved to straddle his lap as her tongue explored and danced with his. Now that she'd begun, she was feverish to touch his skin. She quickly unbuttoned his shirt and splayed her hands across his chest, running her fingers through the coarse hair that grew there.

Grabbing hold of the top of the shirt as it lay against his shoulders, she peeled it from his body then slid her fingers down to his belt buckle. She quickly undid the buckle and unsnapped his jeans, wanting to feel the hardness of him against her skin. She easily released him from the confines of his boxers while running her tongue down the length of his chest and straight to his throbbing penis.

Abby heard him groan as she took the length of him into her hot, moist mouth. Running her tongue around the tip, she sucked and licked as she felt him harden even more.

"Abby, honey, you keep that up and I'm not going to hold out much longer."

"Tonight is about what I want," said Abby as she continued her onslaught.

"Yes, ma'am. It is." Spence smiled for a moment as he relaxed and let his body enjoy the sensations of pleasure she was giving him. Moments later he felt his climax erupt into Abby's beautiful mouth.

"Now," said Abby, "I think we could use a shower before we go to bed and continue doing what I want to do." Abby smiled up at Spence.

"Your wish is definitely my command, my beautiful princess," said Spence as he pulled her up. Standing, he picked her up in his arms and headed for the bathroom.

Standing Abby on the floor for a moment, Spence adjusted the shower spray before allowing her to step inside, closing the door behind them.

Abby was lost in a deluge of sensations assaulting her body. Rivulets of shower water ran down the floor beside her with stray droplets hitting her body here and there.

Spence gently pressed his lips to hers. Abby returned his kiss and demanded entrance with her tongue. He liked this woman. He ravaged her mouth with his tongue and pressed his hardness into her abdomen.

Her senses begged for more with each touch she felt. Spence licked at her nipple and arching her back, she tried hard to thrust the nipple into his hot mouth. More was all she could think about.

When he removed his mouth from that nipple and crossed to the other, she felt a coldness where once the warmth had been. She needed him to take the nipple back into his moist, hot mouth but he was sucking hard on the other one. He immediately covered the abandoned nipple with the palm of his hand moving in a circular motion. The sensations were driving her libido crazy and she needed him inside her to quench her thirst.

Sex with Spence was incredible. He did things to her no one else had never managed.

He covered both nipples with the palms of his hands as he slowly drew a line of kisses down toward her navel and beyond. He parted her lips and slowly inserted two fingers while resting his thumb against her nubbin' and softly began to nip and bite at her outer lips while slowly moving his fingers in and out and ever so gently rubbing her clit in the process.

Abby sighed with ecstasy as she let the sensations take over. She rode the wave to its crest. Her hands found the baldness of his head and slid over it. She wanted to ride the high as long as possible before falling over its edge. His fingers were pushing and rubbing against the front walls of her insides and all of a sudden, she gasped as her climax hit in full force.

Her fingers tightened and she pushed against his mouth, wanting that moment to last a lifetime. Her body tensed, her nipples strained. She could hear someone screaming and it took a full minute before she realized it was her. Every nerve in her body answered her climax.

He continued his thrusting, pushing and rubbing until she was exhausted. Never in her life had she enjoyed a climax more and never had one made her scream with pleasure. This must have been what a couple of her friends were talking about when they discussed the "Big O". She was totally spent. Her legs were too weak to support her body and all she wanted to do now was sleep.

Spence lifted her from the shower floor and laid her on her bed crawling in beside her and pulling the covers up over them.

"Oh, God, that was so wonderful," she whispered.

"Shhhh, love, sleep now."

Spence lay beside her and listened as her breathing steadied to a slow rhythm. This woman was getting under his skin. Actually, when he thought about it, this woman had already gotten under his skin. She'd just slipped in without him ever feeling a thing until it had already happened. And come to think of it, what did he feel?

Who was he kidding? He was so far in love with her, he would cease to exist without her. Tomorrow morning while he was in Tuscaloosa at the training session, he'd stop by the jewelers and pick up a ring for her. He wanted to give her something new and bright. One chosen just for her.

Then, maybe on their first anniversary he could have his mother's wedding ring, the one his dad had given her, made into some sort of anniversary ring for Abby. But for now, he wanted her to have something he would pick just for her.

He had waited a lifetime for this woman. They shared something from a life long ago and now fate had brought them back together. He may not believe in magical mistletoe, but he sure believed in fate.

* * *

Spence had left town early this morning and Abby missed him already. She stood looking out her back door at two deer foraging on the edge of the woods behind her house.

She needed to make an important decision in her life and it was now harder than ever. She'd come back to Shady Rivers to clear her head and instead she'd managed to make it even more confused.

Dang it. She needed a piece of that mistletoe and she was going to get it. If she went now, while Spence was gone, she'd have no choice but to conquer her fear and climb that stupid tree or she'd be stuck up there until Spence returned in the evening.

* * *

Abby crossed the walk into the town square and scurried over to the big basswood tree. Her determination wavered as she looked up at the mistletoe.

"No, you stop that. No backing out, girl. This is your one chance. You can do this. Just keep looking up like Spence said. Keep looking upward." Abby grabbed hold of the first branch.

Taking a deep breath, her gaze upward, she slowly lifted her foot off the ground and placed it on the first low branch, lifting her body upward. A small bead of sweat popped out on her forehead and her heart began a faster beat.

"You can do this. You're okay. Just take a deep breath and remember, you're gonna make it to that little piece of mistletoe. It's not far."

Abby slowly climbed upward one branch at a time, giving herself a pep talk in between each one. Now, she was almost in reach. If she leaned outward just slightly she'd be able to grab the small piece hanging just out of reach.

"Get down from there!" yelled Mike South as he hurried across the square.

Abby startled, lost her hold and her footing and fell screaming to the ground below.

"Damn it, lady," said Mike as he hurried over to Abby and knelt beside her, "Are you hurt?"

"Well, of course, I'm hurt," Abby replied through the tears, "I think I've broken my ankle again. What'd you have to yell at me for? This is all your fault!"

"I wasn't the one up in that tree, now was I? You just lay right there. I'll get Doc Watkins over here and he can check it out." Mike stood up. Glancing around, he spotted Mrs. Tuckerman headed into Katy's.

"Hey, Mrs. Tuckerman," he yelled, "Go get Doc Watkins. Got an emergency over here."

"Oh, lawd! An emergency. I'm on my way as fast as I can." Sarah hurried around the corner toward the doc's small office.

A few minutes later, she burst through the front door, yelling as she went.

"Doc, Doc! You in here. Where in tarnation are you? Mike's got his self one of them emergencies!" she yelled as she continued hurrying towards the back.

Doc Watkins, his gray hair askew, stepped out into the hallway nearly bumping into Sarah.

"What in blazes are you yellin' about, woman?" he asked as he stuck his pen back in his white lab coat.

"Mike's got an emergency over there in the square, by the basswood," she said fanning herself from all the exertion.

"Here, you better sit down and catch your breath. Keep telling you to lay off Miss Becky's cheesecake or you're gonna have a heart attack one of these day."

"Don't talk to me about weight, you ol' coot! You carrying around a few extra tires yourself. Now get your doctoring bag and get on over there. I think somebody fell out of that tree again."

"Well, why didn't you say so in the first place?" He hurried back into his office cubbyhole, grabbed his satchel and headed out the front door. Minutes later he was scampering across the square toward the basswood.

"Hey Doc, good to see you were in."

"Whatcha got here, son?"

"Lady may have a broken ankle. She was climbing the tree and fell."

"You yelled at me and made me fall."

98

"Okay, young lady, let me take a look here."

Doc began a careful examination of Abby's ankle. Feeling for a pedal pulse, he was relieved to find one. Finally, he said, "We're gonna have to get this ankle x-rayed. I don't think it's broken but there could be a hairline fracture so we just need to make sure. Mike, if you'll bring the ambulance around, we'll get her loaded. I'll sit in the back with her and you or Spence'll have to drive."

"Spence is over in Tuscaloosa. I'll drive."

"Okay, I'll stay here with her and you get the ambulance."

"You got it, Doc," said Mike as he headed back to the Sheriff's Office. Minutes later he pulled up beside the square, opened the back door and headed over with the stretcher.

"Wait a minute," said Abby, "that thing looks like the ambulance I rode in when I was a kid."

"Yeah, well, probably is," said Doc. "Ain't nothing wrong with being 'old.' It still works."

"Are you sure?" Abby asked.

"Don't you worry yourself none. It's made the trip many a time and hasn't left a patient on the side of the road yet."

"Well that's good to know. I think," said Abby.

* * *

The trip to Tuscaloosa had been tiring and the pain medication she'd been given by the emergency room doctor for her sprained ankle, left her a little woozy. But Spence had once again come to her rescue. She hadn't known when Mike called him but he'd left his session and came into the

99

emergency room like a momma bear looking for her cub. If she hadn't been in so much pain, it would have been funny.

He'd stayed with her the rest of the time which allowed Doc and Mike to take the town's old ambulance and return to Shady Rivers.

Now, he was fussing over her every move. It was a wonder he was letting her breathe by herself. He helped her into a tub of hot water making sure her ankle was resting comfortably on a pillow he'd taped to the side of the tub to keep if from falling into the water.

He had gotten her a pair of pajamas and had everything ready for her whenever she was ready to get out.

The doorbell rang and Spence pulled the door to the bathroom closed and headed to open the front door.

Opening it, Spence looked down at a man who was a good six inches smaller than himself and probably half his weight. The man reminded Spence of the smart kid in school who sat on the front row and had the answer for any question the teacher asked.

"What can I do for you?" asked Spence.

"This is Three Sixty-two Arlington?"

"Yep, sure is. What can I do for you?"

"I'm looking for Judge Abigail Rutledge."

"She's soaking in a bubble bath right now. What can I do for you?"

"And just how do you know she's in a bubble bath?"

"I put her in it, that's how. Now, I'm going to ask you one more time. What business you got with Abby?"

"I'm her fiancé and my business with her is none of your business. Now, if you'll step aside ..."

Spence stood there for a moment looking at the man standing before him, "What's your name?"

"Preston Abernathy."

"Tell you what, Preston Abernathy, you wait right here and I'll just ask Abby if she has a fiancé by that name," said Spence as he slammed the door in the guy's face and locked the deadbolt with a loud click.

"Hey, open the damn door!" said Preston as he pounded on the door with his fist.

Spence turned and walked back to the bathroom. Standing outside he tapped on the door.

"Yes," said Abby.

"Abby, there's a guy banging on the door. Said his name was Preston Abernathy and that he was your fiancé. What kind of name is Preston Abernathy anyway?"

"Let him in and tell him I'll be right there."

"Okay, but you call me when you're dressed and I'll get you to the couch."

"Okay, it'll take me a few minutes."

"Oh, don't hurry. You might fall or something. I'll keep Preston Abernathy entertained until you're ready." Spence smiled. *This is going to be fun.*

Spence took his time walking to the front door and stood for a minute before unlocking the deadbolt and opening it.

"Abby says you can come in and have a seat on the couch. But I'm to make sure you don't touch anything," said Spence as he stepped back.

101

"Like hell," said Preston as he stepped around Spence, walked into the living room and looked around.

"Sit over there on the couch," said Spence. "Don't touch anything and I'll get Abs."

"Abs? She hates that name."

"Maybe she just don't like the way you say it," replied Spence as he headed down the hallway. "Ever think about that?"

Knocking lightly on the bathroom door, he whispered quietly, "Abby, you dressed?"

"Yes, you can come in now," she replied.

Spence quickly opened the door and stepped inside. Abby sat on the padded bench he'd placed beside the bathtub earlier to make it easier for her to undress and get into the bathtub.

Damn but that woman did things to his insides. She was just as beautiful as she was ornery.

"So, you ready to go figure out if the mistletoe has told you this Abernathy guy is the one for you?"

"I didn't get any mistletoe, remember, but I'm at least ready to go find out what he's doing here," she said as she tied her robe a little tighter.

"You want me to leave or stay?" he asked.

"Well, of course, you can stay if you like. Preston is a nice person. You'll enjoy talking with him," she smiled as Spence bent over and lifted her up in his arms being careful of her ankle.

"Something tells me he's not going to be so friendly tonight," said Spence as he shoved open the bathroom door with his foot. The door swung open and slammed hard into Preston's nose.

"Damn it, son of a bitch, geez," said Preston as he bent over holding his nose. "You've bloodied my fuckin' nose!"

"Oh goodness, Spence, put me down and grab some tissue from the bathroom for Preston."

"Like hell, I will. He can get his own damn tissue and I'm taking you to the recliner, so we can get that ankle propped up like you're supposed to," said Spence as he pushed past Preston. "Suck it up, Buttercup. At least it didn't hit you in the nuts."

"I think you broke my damn nose!"

"Grab yourself some tissue and don't be bleeding on the carpet," Spence yelled back as he headed to the living room with Abby and placed her gently in the recliner. Grabbing the afghan off the sofa arm, he unfolded it and placed it around Abby's lap.

Preston scurried into the bathroom and grabbed some tissue paper off the toilet roll and held it against his nose. "Damn, son of a bitch," he muttered as he headed back to the living room.

"Are you alright?" asked Abby as Preston walked into the living room.

"The better question is what the hell were you doing eavesdropping?" said Spence.

"Abby, honey, would you send this jerkwad back where he belongs. We need to talk."

"Oh, Preston, Spence is okay. We can talk in front of him. What are you doing here, anyway?"

"I brought you a copy of the *Times*. Thought you'd care to read that little article right there," he said as he pointed to an article with her photo attached to it.

"I already know all about that article."

"Well, how do you explain the part about asking some dumb mistletoe to tell you whether or not you can marry me?"

"Don't knock it buster," piped in Spence. "That's magical mistletoe. People come from all over to get a piece of it. If that mistletoe says you ain't marriage material, then you ain't marriage material. Plain and simple."

Abby lowered her face to hide her grin. She knew Spence didn't believe in the tale but he was spouting it off as though it were the gospel. And he was doing it because she believed it. Her heartbeat quickened and a warm sensation slid into home plate. She'd deal with that later.

"Stay out of this, asshole," said Preston. "I bet you're the one who leaked the story to the press in the first place?"

Abby looked at Spence. Her heart skipped a beat. That thought hadn't crossed her mind. Surely, he wouldn't do that to her.

"You'd lose that bet," said Spence. "The people in this town like our mistletoe and we don't take kindly to strangers showing up trying to steal pieces of it or trying to tell us it's not magical. So, if I were you, I'd take that little newspaper of yours and head on back to whatever rock you crawled out from under. You're definitely not welcome in this here town."

"Says who?"

"Says the Sheriff," replied Spence.

"Sheriff? Haven't seen one since I got here."

"You just didn't look hard enough," said Spence as he removed his wallet from his pocket and flipped it open displaying his Sheriff's Badge.

"You two cool the testosterone overload in this room. Preston, Spence *is* the Sheriff here and he would not have told the *Times* about the article. And Spence, neither would Preston. Preston loves me. We've been engaged for five years and we've known each other since I moved to New York. Now you two just quit sniping at each other."

"Abs, honey—"

"Preston! How many times have I asked you not to call me that? I hate it."

"You let him call you Abs and I can't?"

Abby could see the anger flash across Preston's face.

"I do not!" Abby noticed the smirky grin cross Spence's face. "Spence, stop it."

"Hey, I'm just sitting here on the arm of this recliner minding my own business. He's the one causing problems."

"You two are acting like first graders. Act like adults, would you?"

"Abby, honey," said Preston, "we really need to talk and we obviously can't do it with Barney Fife here. Send him home."

"Maybe it's for the best, Spence," said Abby. "I'm okay and if I need anything in the next little while, Preston can get it for me. I'll call you later."

"If he tries anything ..."

"Spence, go home."

Spence reluctantly stood up and walked toward the door.

"You just remember, I'm right next door and I'll be listening for her scream. If she does, I'll be on your ass before you know what happened."

"Spence!"

"I'm going, I'm going. I just want him to know he better not do anything at all to hurt you." Spence walked out and closed the door as he smiled to himself.

* * *

Tossing his keys on the hall table, Spence picked up the receiver on this home phone and dialed a number.

"Hey, Johnson, can you do a favor for me?" asked Spence after dialing the phone.

"Hey, man, sure. Whatcha need?"

"You know that article you did on the Judge and that mistletoe crap?"

"Yeah, got quite a few stars in my cap over that one."

"You know how it got all the way to the *Times*?"

"No, but I saw they picked it up."

"You know anybody there you could call and find out how it got on the front page?"

"Sure. Give me a day or two and I'll get back to you."

"Thanks, man. I'll owe you one. And you owe her one for putting that crap in the paper in the first place."

* * *

"Listen, Abby," said Preston after Spence had left and headed back to his place, "I need to get you back to New York as quickly as we can so we can do damage control on your reputation. The best way to do that is to go ahead and get married as soon as we get back. That way people will see you really don't believe that hogwash about this mistletoe having some kind of magic. They'll realize it was something this podunk town made up."

"I don't know, Preston—"

"You don't have to know, honey. I know. I know what's best for you. You know your grandmother would want you to be happy. If she were here, she'd agree with me."

"We need to talk Preston, but this pain killer is making me sleepy."

"It's okay, honey. You just go ahead and go to sleep. We can talk tomorrow. I'll take care of everything. You just sit back and relax. Sleep will make you feel better. Now, go on to sleep and I'll take care of everything."

* * *

Spence was up early the next morning, walked down into the kitchen to pour himself a cup of coffee. He caught a glimpse of his phone's message light blinking, walked over and pushed the button.

"Hey, Spence, Johnson here. Got the info you wanted. Seems the sister of that Judge's fiancé has a kid going to college over at the University of Alabama. He sent the paper to his mom and I guess she gave it to her brother, the fiancé, and he thought it was funny. He's friends with that reporter. Rest is history. If you need anything else call me back."

Spence pushed replay on the machine just to make sure he'd heard right. Now, what was he going to do with that information? Abby needed to know what type of person she was intending to marry. He just wasn't sure he wanted to be the one to tell her.

CHAPTER FOURTEEN

Abby awoke and felt cramped. She tried to stretch out her legs but her feet hit something that didn't give.

"Oh, you awake?" came a voice.

It took a minute before Abby recognized it as Preston's.

"Where am I?" she asked, her mind still foggy.

"We'll be home in about ten minutes, honey. How's your ankle feeling this morning?"

"Home? Which home? Where are we?" realizing she was in the back seat of Preston's Hummer, Abby sat up and looked around.

"We're about ten minutes away from your house in New York, honey. I took care of everything. Flew us back home in mom's jet and now we're almost back to your place.

"What? I don't want to go to New York, Preston."

"Listen, Abs—"

"How many times do I have to tell you not to call me that, Preston. For once, try listening."

"I'm sorry, honey. I know you're upset about that Sheriff guy leaking that story to the *Times* and I don't blame you."

"What? Spence? Spence would never do that."

"You just don't remember all of last night, honey. You were so groggy from those pain pills. That reporter from New York called you and wanted your take on the story. He told you where he got the story from. It was that Sheriff guy. Remember."

All the air left Abby's lungs. Spence. Spence wouldn't do that to her, would he? Not after all they'd shared. She'd trusted him with her thoughts, her memories. Surely he wouldn't have done that to her.

But, on the other hand, what if he'd done it before he'd gotten to know her. What if he had done it that first night he'd found her stuck up in the tree. He hadn't known her then. Yet, he hadn't told her about it afterwards either.

She just couldn't get her mind around it. Maybe when the pills wore off completely she could think better. She lay back down on the seat and drifted back to sleep.

* * *

Spence dressed and drove over to his office.

"Morning, Sheriff," said Mike as he dropped the chair's legs to the floor, removed his feet from the desk and sat up shuffling papers around on the desk.

"It's alright, son, relax. You're entitled to relax a bit. Can you handle the office a little longer? I need to stop over at Abby's and make sure she's okay, then I have to run to Tuscaloosa for a bit. Should be back here by noon."

110

"Sure thing. I caught a few winks last night while everything was quiet."

"Good. Then I'll see you around noon."

"Sure thing," said Mike.

Spence turned and headed back out the door, jumped back in his truck and headed back toward home. Pulling into his own drive he parked and walked over to Abby's.

Standing on her porch, Spence rang the doorbell and waited. He figured it would take her a few minutes to get to the door. He waited. And waited. Finally, he took hold of the doorknob and turned but it was locked. That was good in Abby's current condition.

Spence banged loudly on the door.

"Abby, it's me, Spence," he yelled.

No answer.

This was not like Abby. If that Preston guy had hurt her ...

Spence walked over to the loose wooden board on the porch's floor. He'd seen Abby do the same thing. Reaching underneath it, he pulled out the hidden key, walked over and unlocked the door before putting the key back in its hiding place.

Opening the door, he yelled out, "Abby, you upstairs?"

He listened. Still no answer.

Spence took off on a run up the stairs. He searched the entire house with no sign of Abby. Her bed had not been slept in either. Spence came to the only conclusion his mind would allow. Preston had taken her back to New York. She would have been too drugged to fight and Abby had already told him that Preston was a take charge kind of guy. He'd just bet money Preston

111

had taken advantage of Abby's condition and hauled her off to New York.

Well, he would just have to go to New York, and haul her right back to Shady Rivers where she belonged. But first he had a couple stops to make.

Pulling up beside the town square, Spence hopped out of his truck and walked over to the basswood tree.

* * *

"Hey, Mike," said Katy as she sat a cup of coffee down on the counter in front of him. "Would you look at that?"

Mike turned to look in the same direction as Katy.

"Damn it. Another climber," said Mike as he stood up.

"Hold on," said Katy, as she reached across the counter grabbing Mike's arm. "You see who that is?"

Mike looked again.

"Damn, is that Spence?"

"It sure is," said Katy, "and in broad open daylight. That man's got it bad."

"Got what bad?" asked Mike.

"You know, you men are just plain dumb as a box of rocks. He's in love. He's in love with Abigail Rutledge. That boy's climbing that damn tree for her."

"Well, Sheriff or not, he can't be climbing that tree. It's against the law."

"You gonna go arrest him, are you?"

"Uh, me, no. No, don't think I want to be wrestling any bears today," said Mike.

"Wise decision," said Katy as she stood there grinning.

CHAPTER FIFTEEN

It was dawn by the time Spence arrived in front of what he hoped was Abby's condo. He was tired from driving all night long but he was determined to be in front of Abby's place by day break.

No one had come or gone since he'd been there and it was now eight o'clock. If Preston was there with her he would have left for work by now. Spence opened the door to his truck and walked up to Abby's door. Pushing the doorbell, he leaned against the door jam and waited.

A few minutes later, he could hear her hobbling footsteps coming toward the door. He breathed a sigh of relief.

Abby opened the door. A look of surprised delight crossed her face.

"You forgot this," said Spence as he handed her a bouquet of mistletoe. The moment she took it, he pulled the door closed.

Abby stood for a second looking down at the mistletoe in her hand. Had he climbed the tree for her and actually driven all the way to New York City just to give it to her. She looked up to realize he'd closed the door. He'd given her the mistletoe and just left without saying anything. She had to catch him before he had time to get back to his truck and leave. She grabbed hold of the knob and jerked the door open. Spence stood there still leaning against the door jam, his arms crossed in front of his chest and his legs crossed at the ankles.

"So," he said, "I see you have a twig or two of that magical mistletoe and since I'm the first guy you've seen, does that mean you'll marry me?"

Abby stood there as tears filled her eyes.

"You know, my grandmother always told me whenever I was looking for the man I was meant to be with, I could find him with a piece of this magical mistletoe. And since you're the only man around, I guess that means that I should marry you." Abby smiled up at him.

"Do you think this might help you make up your mind?" said Spence as he pulled a little blue box out of his pocket and opened it in front of her.

"Oh, Spence, it's the most beautiful thing I've ever seen!'

"Is that a yes, then?" he asked.

"Yes, yes, a thousand times yes!" said Abby as she threw her arms around him and hobbled closer.

"Careful," said Spence, "we don't want to hurt that ankle." He picked her up and carried her inside, shutting the door with his foot. "You want to get married today or tomorrow? Or we could fly to Hawaii if you want."

"If it's okay with you, I think I'd like to get married in Shady Rivers. New York is okay but Shady Rivers is home."

"I was hoping you'd say that. How about a Spring wedding right there in the town square?"

"Oh, I'd love that. Do you think we could?"

"Sure and I'll bet we can get some of the guys to bring out their dulcimers and things and play a little music for us."

"Oh my gosh, really?"

"Anything you want, you just name it and it's yours."

"Well, right now, the one thing I want is you."

Spence leaned over and kissed her lips as the doorbell rang.

"You expecting company?" asked Spence.

"It's probably Preston. I had called him and told him to come over because I had a few things to discuss with him."

"I'm not going anywhere," said Spence.

"No, I don't' want you to. I'd rather you stay here with me. What I have to say to him isn't going to be pleasant and I'd rather have someone here to make sure I'm okay."

"If he even looks like he's gonna touch you, I'll have him out the door so fast he won't know whether he's coming or going," said Spence as he sat her down on the sofa and placed her ankle on a pillow. "I'll get the door."

Spence walked over and opened the door. As he stood there blocking Preston's entry, he watched as a myriad of expressions crossed Preston's face. The look of total and utter surprise was priceless as far as Spence was concerned.

"What can I do for you?" asked Spence.

"What are you doing here?" asked Preston as he tried to peer around Spence.

"I could ask you the same thing."

"Abby called me. She and I need to talk about our plans. We're getting married and you just need to go back to Podunk City, Barney—"

"Before you finish that sentence, I'd think about it long and hard if I were you," said Spence as he straightened himself even taller.

"See here now," said Preston, "don't go getting all Sheriffy on me. Where's Abby? She called me and wanted me to come right over."

"That she did. I believe the lady has some things to talk to you about. Go right on in there," said Spence as he stepped aside. "But keep in mind, that I'll be right beside her."

"To hell you will," muttered Preston as he stepped inside and headed to the living room. "Abby, Abby, honey, are you okay? He hasn't hurt you has he. I'll call the police and have him arrested if he's so much as looked at you the wrong way."

"No, Preston, Spence hasn't hurt me at all," she said as she smiled up at Spence as he sat down on the sofa's arm next to her.

"Alright then, send him on his way and we can get started talking about our plans," said Preston as he sat down in the armchair across from the sofa. "Look, I brought all the brochures for you to look at to pick out a place for our honeymoon."

Preston spread the brochures on the coffee table between them and smiled at Abby.

"First, Preston, Spence isn't going anywhere. I asked him to stay."

"Why would you do that?" Preston asked as he picked up one of the brochures. "I was thinking France might be nice," he said as he opened the brochure and laid it out in front of her.

"Preston, are you even listening to me?" asked Abby.

"Of course, I am. I'm waiting for you to give me an answer about France. Paris, in particular."

"No, no you haven't heard me at all. You're too busy taking charge of whatever, you don't even take the time to actually listen. The problem with Paris is that I'm not going. I'm not going to France either. I'm not going anywhere with you because I'm not marrying you."

"Has this fool drugged you or something?" asked Preston.

Abby saw the look of disbelief cross his face.

"No, you're the one who drugged me, Preston. You gave me more of those pain pills, didn't you? You gave me more of them so you could drag me out of my house and into your plane and get me all the way back here to New York with very little fuss."

"No, Abby, honey—"

"Don't you Abby honey me anything. To think that I was considering marrying you at one point. And then to realize you'd do something like that to me makes my skin crawl."

"Listen, Abs—"

"No, you listen to me. I've warned you about calling me Abs. Yet you continue to do it because it's what you want and not what I want. Now it's time for you to pay close attention to what I'm going to tell you because I'm not going to say it twice."

"Abby, honey, just let me—"

"No, Preston. I want you out of my house, and out of my life. I'm sure you can find your way to the door."

"Before you go though," said Spence, "I think there's something you need to tell Abby about."

"I don't take orders from you," said Preston as he stood up from the chair.

"Oh, this time, I think you will," said Spence as he stood up, towering over Preston. "See, there's this little issue about a newspaper article."

"I had nothing to do with that and you can't prove otherwise."

"Well, now, I wouldn't be so sure of that," said Spence as he pulled out his cell phone. "Shall I make a little phone call and see what we can find out?"

"It doesn't matter anyway," said Preston as he turned back to Abby. "I'll call you tomorrow, Abby, when this jerk isn't around and we can talk."

"Don't call me, Preston. If you do, I'll issue a restraining order against you and I'll just bet the same reporter who printed the article about me would be delighted to print that little tidbit, too."

"You're going to regret this, Abby. Any woman would jump at the chance to be Mrs. Preston Abernathy," he said as he turned and headed for the door.

"Well, hopefully, she'll deserve you," said Abby as she watched him leave.

"You, okay, hon," asked Spence as he sat down beside Abby.

"Yeah, I'll be fine. I'm just so mad right now I could bite nails into."

"Tell you what, sweetheart. Let me fix you a cup of hot tea. We can sit here in front of the fireplace and relax for a bit. Then, if you'd like, I can call the movers and have 'em come in and pack you up. We could head back home as soon as they've got your stuff loaded onto a truck."

"You know, that sounds wonderful to me. The sooner I'm away from here, the better I'll like it."

CHAPTER SIXTEEN

Spring had finally arrived. Abby could hardly wait to become Mrs. Spencer Cartwright. They had already decided to sell Spence's house since it had no sentimental attachment. That had been Spence's idea. Abby thought it made sense and besides she loved her grandmother's house. She'd grown up there and it'd be fun to raise their children there. She'd wanted a house full and Spence promised he'd try his best to accommodate her on creating them.

Now, she was another nervous bride waiting for her cue to walk from Flo's Beauty Boutique, across the town square to the little gazebo where the ceremony would be performed.

Sarah Tuckerman had made Abby a beautiful bridal bouquet of apple blossoms picked from the trees in Sarah's own yard. Her wedding gown was the same one her mother had worn for her own wedding.

Elmer Shelton and his band played songs on their dulcimers, banjos, fiddles and other wonderful instruments Abby remembered from her childhood days. She had missed the sound of sweet strings living in the Big Apple.

Everything was ready and Abby heard the sound of the Bridal March begin to play. Opening the door of Flo's, she saw Doc Watkins waiting on the sidewalk to escort her down the flowered path to the gazebo.

Abby reached over and took his arm.

"Ready my dear?" asked Doc.

"Sure am, Doc," she replied.

"Before we start, I want to give you this," he said as he pulled out a tissue and carefully unfolded it revealing a tiny blue topaz cross on a silver chain.

"Oh my gosh, that's so beautiful!" exclaimed Abby.

"I want you to have it. I have a little secret that goes with that cross and if you promise not to tell anybody, I'll tell it to you," said Doc as he winked at her.

"Oh, I promise. Tell me," she said.

"I bought that cross years ago for a lady I was in love with. Here let me put it around your neck."

"But I thought you were never married, Doc."

"That's right. I haven't been. See the lady was in love with someone else, so I never told her. I kept the little necklace though, you know, just in case."

"You've never told her all these years?"

"No, I never did. She's gone now."

"Oh, that's so sad."

"No, no, I didn't tell you that to make you sad, I told you because I wanted you to know I had bought that necklace for your mother."

"My mother? You were in love with my mother?"

"Yes, I was. Still am. I just wanted you to know that nothing would please me anymore than to give this to you."

Abby stood there for a moment looking at the necklace.

"Doc are you trying to—"

"Oh heavens to Betsy, no. No child. If you're trying to ask me if I'm your father, no sirree. Your mother never would have ... I mean, she never even knew. Nobody knew. I was just a shy, bashful kid back then. I just wanted to share my secret with someone before my time came and I thought there was nobody I'd rather share it with than someone else who loved her, too."

"Then, thank you, Doc. I'm so glad you did. I'll cherish this necklace as much as you have all these years. We'll both love her together from now on. And your secret is safe with me."

"I thought it would be. Now, enough indulging an ol' codger. Let's get on across the street. You've got a mighty handsome groom waiting for you, I believe."

"Yes, I do," said Abby as she again took hold of Doc's arm and the two began to walk toward the gazebo.

Their travels were soon interrupted as Tiny came ambling down the street sniffing the air. He passed the bakery and the second-hand shop just in time to catch Abby and Doc as they got to the middle of the street. Tiny stuck his nose in the air and sniffed.

"What in tarnation's got Tiny's interest?" said Abby as the bison continued to sniff the air.

"Usually it's Katy's fried apple pies," said Doc.

At that moment, Abby, Doc and Tiny, realized what had caught Tiny's interest, as the big bison took that moment to chomp down on Abby's Apple Blossom bridal bouquet.

"Nooooooo," yelled Abby. "That was mine, Tiny."

"It's alright," said Doc. "Let him have it and he'll go on his way. Here, take my lapel rose. Won't be as pretty but it'll work."

"Yeah, you're right. Thanks, Doc. Hopefully, nothing else'll go wrong before we get across the street," said Abby as she smiled at the rose in her hand.

"It'll still be a memorable wedding."

"That it will be. Let's hurry before the band gets tired and needs a break," said Abby as she smiled at Doc.

The two hurried across the street and into the town square. Abby stepped into her place beside Spence standing in the gazebo. She had to laugh when Spence leaned over and whispered in her ear.

"It's magic," he said as he handed her another piece of magical mistletoe.

"But you don't believe in magic," she whispered back.

"Maybe I've changed my mind," he said as he took her hand and turned back to face the minister as the ceremony began.

* * *

If you enjoyed this book, please leave an honest review.

One of the best and easiest things you can do after purchasing a novel is to leave reviews. Not just one but many on different sites.

The reviews on Goodreads are seen by the super-passionate-uber-book-fans which is fantastic but your average everyday online book shopper heads to a place to actually "buy" the book like Amazon or B&N. So when you leave a review on Amazon or B&N, you are increasing the book's chance of being bought by those shoppers.

By leaving reviews on as many sites as you can find, you increase the book's *'you may also like'* algorithms. Those algorithms consider a book's popularity when making suggestions to potential consumers. Therefore, the more reviews a book has simply gives more potential for exposure.

Also, what is more enticing to you: a book with three reviews or the book with three-hundred? So help Maggie by posting reviews on numerous sites.

Thanks to all who leave reviews on Maggie's books. She appreciates them all!

COMING SOON!

12 Other Stories in the Shady Rivers Series

Shady Rivers is a fictional small town in my home state of Alabama. With some quirky characters and a big secret, you'll come to love the town and its inhabitants. There's Colonel Bueford T. Beauregard, III, a ghost who hangs around the town's bar and Bubba, the big dude who rides a Harley and finds out the love of his life, Jonette, was a he before he became a she. Find out who or what keeps stealing apple pies from Katy's Kitchen and who saves a teacup chihuahua named Pinky.

Coming soon! Visit my website at www.maggierivers.com and sign up for my newsletter and be among the first to know when the next book in the Shady Rivers series is released.

Much love to you all!

Contact **Maggie** at:

P.O. Box 4601
Des Moines, IA 50305

Or by email at maggie@maggierivers.com

Visit Maggie's website at:
http://www.maggierivers.com

Chat with us on Facebook:
https://www.facebook.com/maggierivers-author/

To order a personally autographed copy of any of
Maggie's books contact Maggie through any of
the above.

If you'd like Maggie to come to your town for a
book signing, a book club meeting, a festival or
any other event you might be planning, just call
(515-299-5100) or email for details.

Maggie also writes as one of The Stiletto Girls. Check out these books with three stories in each!

BOOKS BY
The Stiletto Girls

133

Spurs and Stilettos

Glenna West, C. Deanne Rowe,
Magnolia 'Maggie' Rivers

Help Maggie Make the Best Seller Lists!

Just how can you help Maggie Rivers make the best seller lists without going bankrupt yourself? Here are a few suggestions.

1. **Post reviews to major retail sites.**

   One of the best and easiest things you can do after purchasing a novel is to leave a review. Not just one but many on different sites. The reviews on Goodreads are seen by the super-passionate-uber-book-fans which is fantastic but your average everyday online book shopper heads to a place to actually "buy" the book like Amazon or B&N. So when you leave a review on Amazon or B&N, you are increasing the book's chance of being bought by those shoppers. By leaving reviews on as many sites as you can find, you increase the book's *'you may also like'* algorithms. Those algorithms consider a book's popularity when making suggestions to potential consumers. Therefore, the more reviews a book has simply gives more potential for exposure. Also, what is more enticing to you: a book with three reviews or the book with three-hundred? So help your team by posting reviews on numerous sites.

2. **Tell others about the book.**
   Mention the books to everyone—friends, family, your social media. Word-of-mouth is huge and just talking about a title you loved can have a ripple effect. Someone picks it up because you were so enthusiastic about it. It's said that each person knows 250 people. You tell your 250, they tell their 250 who then tell their 250. And so on and so forth!

3. **Gift the book.**
   Books make wonderful gifts and you have the opportunity to have them autographed which makes them extra special! Keep several copies on hand to give for a birthday/holiday or just an "I thought of you." Authors are always grateful for extra sales!

4. **Donate a copy**.
   What do you do with your copy once it's read? If it's not something you intend to read again donate it to your local library or women's shelter. Leave a copy at your doctor's/dentist's office. If you loved the book so much you can't part with it (which we certainly hope is the case with our books), then consider buying a second copy specifically for your library. Either way ensures new readers will continue to find the title! If they like it, they'll head out to find more books by that same author.

5. **Read the book in public.**
   Or at least pretend you are. Take a physical copy and flaunt it in public places—the coffee shop, the park, the bus ride to/from work. Book lovers notice what other folks read, and someone might purchase a copy because they saw you.

6. **Recommend the title to booksellers.**
   Knowing readers are interested in a title puts it on a bookseller's radar. They might order a few copies.

7. **Place it on library hold.**
   When you don't see a book on your library's shelves, put a hold on the title through their catalog system. They'll get a copy and let you know when it arrives!

8. **Place copies on your car's dashboard.**

While you're out shopping, let your car do the advertising. Place your copies of an author's book across your car's dashboard. Back into the parking space so people walking by will see the display!

9. **Place a copy on your desk at work.**
Purchase a book stand and place it on your work desk. Showcase a different book each day. Co-workers may stop by each morning to see what's new.

Help support Maggie and together, we can make the New York Times' Best Seller list!

Thanks to all who leave reviews. I appreciate each and every one!

A HUGE THANK YOU!

I would like to thank you to each and every one of you who purchased my book.

You picked up my book, bought it and are right now sitting in your favorite place about to begin reading a story I created for your reading pleasure. So, yes, thank you from the bottom of my heart!

It is my hope, once you start reading this story, you absolutely cannot put it down until you reach "The End."

But really, I just appreciate the fact you've spent your hard-earned dollars purchasing one of my books. I appreciate you, my readers, whether this is the first book of mine you've purchased or your fourth or fifth.

So, yes, a gigantic thank you. I hope you enjoy it reading as much as I enjoyed writing it for you!

Love,

Maggie

P.S. I hope to meet you all in person someday!

A TRIBUTE TO MY MILITARY BROTHERS AND SISTERS

Photo Courtesy of Jennifer Wright
Carrollton, Texas

"This table is reserved to honor our missing comrades in arms. The tablecloth is white — symbolizing the purity of their motives when answering the call of duty. The single red rose, displayed in a vase, reminds us of the life of each of the missing and their loved ones and friends of these Americans who keep the faith, awaiting answers. The vase is tied with a yellow ribbon, a symbol of our continued determination to account for our missing. A pinch of salt symbolizes the tears endured by those missing and their families who seek answers. A slice of lemon on the plate reminds us of their bitter fate. The Bible represents the strength gained through faith to sustain those lost from our country, founded as one nation under God. The glass is inverted — to symbolize their inability to share this evening's toast. The chair is empty — they are missing."

Author Unknown.

BIOGRAPHY

MAGNOLIA "MAGGIE" RIVERS

A Southern girl born and bred, I began writing as a child, and sold my first piece of writing at the age of twenty-one.

Growing up, I spent as much of my time with books as I could. I still love that first smell of a book as you open its pages and the wonderful feel of it in your hands. Like most writers, my house is filled with books I've read countless times. I could open my own library!

I collect stilettos of all kinds and have them sitting on every available space in my office. They tend to show up in a lot of my novels as does my micro-mini teacup Chihuahua named "Mouse". Believe me though, she's no mouse. I should have named her "Killer" instead!

I write hot, sexy, sizzling romances where the hero is just what my heroine needs. He's strong and confident with broad shoulders, six-pack abs and a pleasure trail that just won't quit. His face is more rugged than handsome, but he has a heart of gold hidden underneath all his protective armor.

Visit Maggie's website at:
http://www.maggierivers.com